"To my family, whose unwavering love and support have been my foundation, and to my friends, who have filled my life with laughter, encouragement, and inspiration. This book is a tribute to the joy and strength you bring to my journey."

THE ECHOES OF SILENT SEPARATION

IN ANOTHER WORLD I'LL BE WAITING

KAHEF TAUQEER

Made with ♥ on the Notion Press Platform
www.notionpress.com

Contents

Foreword

Stories have the power to transport us to times and places that feel both distant and deeply familiar. Zainab and Aayan is one such tale—a poignant melody set against the backdrop of one of history's most tumultuous periods, the partition era.

This novel is not merely about the events of the partition but about the hearts that beat, broke, and endured through its chaos. It's a story of Zainab, a woman torn between societal obligations and the whispers of her soul, and Aayan, whose love remains an unyielding force despite time, distance, and impossible odds.

Through the lens of Zainab and Aayan's journey, the book delves into universal themes of love, sacrifice, and resilience, illuminating the ways in which the human spirit fights to preserve hope even amidst despair. It is a story for anyone who has ever loved deeply, faced loss, or grappled with the complexities of duty and desire.

As you read, you will not only witness the characters' struggles but feel their emotions, walk alongside them through the chaos of partition, and ultimately reflect on how love—both its triumphs and its tragedies—has the power to transcend boundaries.

This tale is a tribute to the enduring spirit of love and a reminder that, even in the harshest of times, some bonds can never be broken. I hope this story resonates with you as deeply as it did with me.

Preface

Writing Zainab and Aayan has been a deeply personal and emotional journey. Set against the backdrop of the tumultuous partition era, this story is more than a historical account—it is a reflection on love, loss, and the complex choices that shape our lives. The idea for this book came to me as I pondered the question of how love can endure, even when circumstances seem to tear it apart. Zainab and Aayan's story is a tribute to the enduring power of love, even in the face of overwhelming adversity.

The characters of Zainab and Aayan have been shaped by my desire to explore the tension between societal expectations and the deep, unspoken bonds that define our most intimate relationships. Zainab is a woman caught between duty and her heart's true desires, and Aayan is the embodiment of hope, willing to cross any boundary to reunite with the woman he loves. Their story is a reflection of the struggles many of us face in choosing between the paths that life imposes on us and the paths our hearts wish to follow.

While the partition itself was a defining event in history, the emotions, sacrifices, and personal stories within this narrative transcend any one time or place. Writing this book was not only a way for me to give voice to the struggles and triumphs of those affected by the partition, but also to remind us all of the strength of the human spirit and how, even amidst chaos, some love stories remain unbroken.

I am immensely grateful to my family and friends for their encouragement and patience as I worked through the challenges of writing this book. Your support has been a constant source of strength. To my readers, I hope that as you read Zainab and Aayan, you find yourselves drawn into the emotional journey of these characters and reflect on the ways in which love shapes our lives and transcends time.

Thank you for allowing me to share this story with you. I hope that it resonates with you long after you've turned the final page.

Acknowledgements

Expressing profound gratitude to my parents, Tauqeer Azam and Tabassum Tauqeer, and my family, whose unwavering support has been my strength throughout this journey. Their belief in me has fueled my creativity and perseverance. Their love and encouragement have lifted me during the toughest times and celebrated with me during successes.

A heartfelt thanks to my dear friend, Suryanshi Shrivastava, for her unyielding support and companionship in completing my first novel. Your insights, patience, and constant motivation have inspired me to reach new heights. This achievement is as much yours as it is mine.

Finally, I am deeply thankful to my brother and sister for their continuous encouragement and understanding. Together, you all have been my strength and my source of inspiration.

Prologue

The bustling streets of Lahore carried a rhythm all their own—a cacophony of clattering rickshaws, vibrant chatter, and the melodic calls of street vendors hawking their wares. Beneath the surface of this vibrant city, however, lay whispers of change, a growing tension that threatened to fracture its delicate harmony. Amid the swirling tides of history stood two souls—Zainab and Ayaan—united by a love that defied tradition and circumstance.

Zainab, a girl with dreams that soared beyond the confines of her traditional upbringing, had found an unexpected solace in Ayaan. The humble craftsman, whose hands wove stories into intricate jewelry, had captured her heart with his open mind and tender spirit. Their stolen moments amidst the chaos of Lahore's marketplaces were a haven, a rebellion against the world that sought to divide them.

Yet, the world beyond their haven was unraveling. Whispers of partition had grown into roars, and the once-bustling streets began to echo with fear and uncertainty. Families were torn apart, lives uprooted, and the dream of a united land crumbled into dust. Amid this turmoil, Zainab and Ayaan's love was a fragile flame, flickering against the winds of fate.

Fate, however, can be a cruel master. Promises whispered under moonlit skies and plans crafted in quiet corners were no match for the storms that loomed ahead. As their city was carved into pieces, so too were their dreams. They made vows to stand by each other, to fight for their love against insurmountable odds. But destiny had other plans.

What unfolded was a tale of heartbreak and resilience, of bonds tested and broken by forces beyond their control. It is a story of love that blossomed in a time of despair, of a connection so profound that it defied even death. As Lahore burned, so did the lives of its people, their stories etched into the fabric of history—unspoken, yet unforgettable.

In the echoes of silent separation, one can still hear the whispers of Zainab and Ayaan—a testament to love's enduring power and the pain of what might have been. Their story is not just theirs but a reflection of thousands torn apart by the tides of history, a haunting reminder of the cost of division and the fragility of hope in the face of darkness.

ONE

The Meeting

The bustling streets of Lahore were alive with the sounds of vendors calling out their wares, the clatter of rickshaws, and the vibrant chatter of its people. Amidst this

cacophony, Zainab, with her dupatta fluttering in the wind, wove through the marketplace, her mind set on the list of items she needed to buy. The scents of spices, incense, and freshly baked bread mingled in the air, creating a heady aroma that was both familiar and comforting.

Zainab had ventured out of her home, a rare occurrence given her family's strict adherence to traditional values. Her father believed in keeping women hidden from the public eye, but with the secret support of her mother, Zainab had managed to pursue her education. This rare trip to the marketplace was under the guise of running

errands, a small taste of the freedom she so deeply craved.

As she approached a small, unassuming trinket stall, her eyes were drawn to the intricate designs of handmade jewelry displayed on a wooden table. The craftsman behind the table, Ayaan, looked up, his eyes meeting hers with a spark of curiosity. He had a warm, inviting smile that instantly put her at ease.

"Assalamualaikum," he greeted her, his voice a soothing contrast to the chaos around them. **"Walaikumassalam,"** Zainab replied, her heart inexplicably fluttering.

Zainab carefully picked up a delicate bracelet adorned with tiny, colorful beads.

"These are beautiful," she said, her fingers tracing the intricate patterns.

Ayaan nodded, his pride evident. "I make them myself. Each piece tells a story, crafted with care and love."

As they spoke, a gentle breeze rustled through the marketplace, carrying with it the promise of something new and exciting. Their conversation flowed easily, and for a brief moment, the world around them faded away.

The marketplace began to fill with the vibrant colors of the evening, the lights twinkling like a thousand stars. Zainab felt a sense of peace she hadn't known in a long time. But little did she realize, this brief encounter would be the

beginning of a love story marked by both beauty and heartache, set against the turbulent backdrop of a nation on the brink of division.

Zainab returned home that evening, the bracelet a reminder of her unexpected encounter. She couldn't help but smile as she remembered Ayaan's kind eyes and gentle voice. The seed of their bond had been planted, and despite the uncertainty that loomed over their world, hope began to blossom in her heart.

Days turned into weeks, and Zainab found herself returning to the marketplace, drawn by an invisible force. Each visit brought new conversations with Ayaan, and their bond grew stronger. She learned about his open-minded views, a

stark contrast to her traditional upbringing. They shared dreams, hopes, and fears, finding solace in each other's company amidst the rising political tensions.

Their meetings became a haven in the midst of the growing unrest. The world outside was changing rapidly, with whispers of partition growing louder. Yet, in the small marketplace, time stood still for Zainab and Ayaan. They made a pact to stand by each other, no matter the challenges ahead. But as the dark clouds of separation loomed, their hearts ached with the uncertainty of what the future held.

Their bond continued to deepen with each stolen moment. Ayaan often surprised Zainab with small gifts—an intricately carved wooden box, a poem written in delicate script, or a flower tucked into the pages of a book. Each gesture was a testament to the growing affection between them. Their conversations became longer, filled with laughter, shared stories, and silent Promises . Each gesture was a testament to the growing affection between them. Their conversations became longer, filled with laughter, shared stories, and silent promises.

Sometimes, Ayaan would leave a handwritten letter for Zainab at the trinket stall, a sweet secret only they shared. These notes became treasures to Zainab, hidden away from prying eyes. On rare occasions, they would meet just beyond the marketplace, sharing a meal in the quiet corners of the city, savoring each other's company away from the watchful eyes of their families.

One afternoon, Ayaan offered Zainab a vibrant flower, its petals delicate against

her skin. "For you," he whispered, his eyes filled with unspoken emotions.

Zainab accepted it with a shy smile, her heart soaring with each small act of affection. Fear of discovery always loomed over their stolen moments. Zainab's family would never approve of her meetings with Ayaan. The secrecy only made their bond stronger, a shared rebellion against the constraints of their world.

On a particularly warm evening, Zainab and Ayaan found a secluded spot by the river, hidden from the bustling city. The setting sun cast a golden hue over the water, creating a serene backdrop for their secret rendezvous.

As they sat together, Ayaan gently reached for Zainab's hand. The warmth of his touch sent a shiver down her spine. "I wish we could share this moment without fear," he whispered, his voice tinged with longing.

Zainab nodded, her heart heavy with the weight of their circumstances. "If only things were different," she murmured, looking into his eyes.

Despite the looming shadows of societal expectations and political unrest, their love continued to grow in these hidden moments. They found joy in the

simplest of things—a shared meal, a walk through the quiet streets at dusk, or a whispered conversation under the stars. Each stolen moment was a defiance of the boundaries that sought to keep them apart.

The fear of being discovered never left them, but it also added an intensity to their bond. They cherished every second, knowing that each encounter could be their last. And with each day that passed, their love deepened, becoming an unbreakable part of their identities.

One evening, as the monsoon rains began to pour, Zainab and Ayaan found themselves seeking shelter under the awning of a small, deserted tea stall. The rain created a curtain around them, isolating them from the rest of the world. The rhythmic sound of raindrops hitting the ground added a magical quality to the moment.

Ayaan, noticing Zainab's slight shiver, took off his shawl and gently draped it over her shoulders. "Here, this should keep you warm," he said softly, his eyes filled with concern.

Zainab looked up at him, her heart swelling with gratitude and affection. "Thank you," she whispered, her voice barely audible over the rain.

They stood close, the warmth of Ayaan's shawl and the intimacy of the moment creating a cocoon of safety and love. Ayaan reached into his pocket and pulled out a small, folded piece of paper. "I wrote something for you," he said, handing it to her with a shy smile.

Zainab unfolded the paper to find a beautifully written poem, each word resonating with the depth of Ayaan's feelings.

The rain fell in a steady, relentless rhythm, the drops soaking the earth beneath their feet as Zainab stood there, the letter trembling in her hands. She had just read the words, and now, with the weight of Ayaan's confession pressing on her heart, she looked up at him, her eyes glistening in the soft glow of the streetlamp.

Ayaan stood just a few steps away, drenched, his heart exposed in the silence that surrounded them. His eyes were locked on hers, waiting, hoping for something he couldn't fully explain, but the moment stretched on like the storm itself—unpredictable, heavy, and full of meaning.

Zainab's voice finally broke the silence, soft and unsteady. She spoke slowly, almost as if trying to digest every word, her voice caught in the rain and the weight of his confession.

“Ayaan...” she whispered, the name hanging between them like a fragile thread. “I... I didn’t know.”

Her words felt like a confession too—one that was caught somewhere between surprise and realization. She unfolded the letter, staring down at it once more, as if the words might change if she looked closely enough. But they didn’t. The truth was clear, written in his honest hand, soaked by the rain but still burning with emotion.

“I never imagined...” she continued, her voice faltering, "that you felt this way."

The rain seemed to pause around them, a brief silence before the storm began anew. Zainab looked back up at Ayaan, her heart heavy with the realization of how much she had taken for granted. She saw him—not just the man standing before her drenched in the downpour, but the one who had carried his feelings for so long in silence, the one who had loved her quietly from the shadows.

“I...” Zainab stepped closer, the rain plastering her hair to her face, her hands shaking as she reached out to him, unsure of what to say or how to respond.

Ayaan stood motionless, his heart in his throat, waiting for the inevitable words that would shape the future they might or might not share.

But instead of words, she closed the distance between them, the letter still clutched in her hands. Gently, she reached up and tucked a wet strand of hair behind his ear, her fingers trembling from the cold and the truth she hadn’t yet admitted to herself.

For a long moment, the world around them faded. There was only the rain, the unspoken confession, and the storm inside their hearts.

Then, quietly, she whispered, "I didn’t know, Ayaan... but maybe I do now."

And for the first time, in the midst of the rain, Ayaan felt the weight of her gaze—full of uncertainty, but also something more. Something that could change everything between them, as the storm raged on.

Tears welled up in her eyes as she read the heartfelt verses. "This is beautiful," she said, her voice choked with emotion.

Ayaan gently wiped away her tears, his touch tender and reassuring. "I meant every word," he said, his voice filled with sincerity.

In that rare, stolen moment, surrounded by the rain and the fading light of the day, Zainab and Ayaan's bond grew even stronger. They knew that their love was a precious gift, one that they would cherish and protect, no matter the challenges that lay ahead.

Their meetings became a haven in the midst of the growing unrest. The world outside was changing rapidly, with whispers of partition growing louder. Yet, in the small marketplace, time stood still for Zainab and Ayaan. They made a pact to stand by each other, no matter the challenges ahead. But as the dark clouds of separation loomed, their hearts ached with the uncertainty of what the future held . Zainab's home life was becoming increasingly difficult. Her family's financial condition was precarious, and her father had started to pressurising her into marrying a wealthy man, Farhan, who was known for his heavy drinking.

The thought of such a marriage filled Zainab with dread, but she felt trapped by her family's expectations and their dire financial need.

Each day, the weight of her family's demands grew heavier, and the moments she spent with Ayaan became her only refuge. In their secret meetings, she found strength and courage to face the harsh realities of her home life. But the fear of losing Ayaan, of being forced into a loveless marriage, haunted her every step.

When Zainab allowed herself a moment of introspection, she dreamed of a partner who was caring and understanding, someone who respected her ambitions and intellect. She yearned for a love built on mutual respect and shared dreams, not one dictated by financial convenience or societal expectations. In Ayaan, she saw glimpses of the person she desired—a man who valued her thoughts and feelings, who supported her quest for knowledge and freedom.

These thoughts filled her with both hope and despair. Hope, because she had found someone like Ayaan. Despair, because the obstacles standing in their way seemed insurmountable. But even in the darkest moments, the memory of their shared smiles and whispered conversations gave her the strength to continue fighting for the life and love she truly wanted.

Every time Zainab met Ayaan, their connection deepened. They shared stolen moments filled with laughter, dreams, and the soft whisper of a love that felt both forbidden and eternal. One evening, under the moonlit sky, Ayaan handed Zainab a small, handwritten letter. "For you," he said, his voice low and tender.

Zainab's heart pounded as she unfolded the letter, Ayaan's elegant script revealing a heartfelt message that spoke of his growing affection for her. Tears welled up in her eyes as she read his words, each sentence resonating with the emotions she, too, had struggled to contain.

The days passed, each one bringing new challenges and the ever-present fear of discovery. Yet, despite the mounting pressure from her family to marry Farhan, Zainab found solace and strength in her love for Ayaan. She cherished the small, romantic moments they shared—like the time he surprised her with a flower tucked into the pages of a book, or the secret meals they enjoyed together in hidden corners of the city.

As the political situation grew more tense, their meetings became even more precious. Every whispered conversation and every shared smile felt like a defiance against the world trying to tear them apart. And though the road

ahead was fraught with uncertainty, Zainab and Ayaan knew that their love was something worth fighting for.

As tensions grew at home, Zainab's family became more vocal about their disapproval. Every time she wanted to step outside, she faced a barrage of taunts and criticisms.

"Going out again? What could be so important?" her father would scoff. Her mother, although more supportive, remained silent, fearing the consequences of defiance.

Among Zainab's few confidants was her childhood friend, Ayesha. Understanding the complexities of Zainab's feelings, Ayesha often covered for her, providing alibis and moral support. "You deserve happiness, Zainab. Don't let them dictate your life," she would whisper, encouraging her to pursue her heart's desires.

On Ayaan's side, his best friend, Sameer, played a crucial role. An open-minded and loyal companion, Sameer understood the depth of Ayaan's love for Zainab. "Don't give up on her," Sameer would say. "Love like yours is rare, and worth every risk."

One evening, as Zainab was preparing to leave for another secret meeting with Ayaan, her brother sneered, "Running off to see your books again, are you? Always pretending to be something you're not."

Zainab took a deep breath, pushing back the tears. She knew that every step she took towards Ayaan was a step towards the life she longed for.

TWO

The Storm

The vibrant streets of Lahore began to change as whispers of partition grew louder. The marketplace, once bustling with life and color, now carried a tension that was impossible to ignore. The air was thick with unease, each day bringing new uncertainties. Amidst this, Zainab and Ayaan's love continued to blossom, an island of hope amidst a sea of chaos.

One evening, as Zainab approached the trinket stall, she noticed a group of men arguing heatedly nearby. Their voices were raised, anger and fear evident in their words. Ayaan was already there, his expression serious as he watched the scene unfold. He caught Zainab's eye and gave her a reassuring smile, but she could see the worry etched on his face.

"Stay close," he whispered as she reached his side. "Things are getting worse."

Zainab nodded, her heart pounding. The threat of violence felt more real than ever before. Despite the danger, she found solace in Ayaan's presence. They walked together through the marketplace, their hands brushing against each other as if to remind themselves of the bond they shared.

As they turned a corner, a commotion erupted behind them. Zainab spun around just in time to see a group of men tearing down a stall, their faces contorted with rage. The crowd scattered, fear spreading like wildfire.

Ayaan pulled Zainab into a narrow alleyway, shielding her with his body as

chaos unfolded around them. "We need to leave, now," Ayaan whispered urgently. Holding Zainab's hand, he led her through a maze of narrow

alleyways, each step further distancing them from the rising turmoil. The sounds of chaos faded, replaced by their ragged breaths and pounding hearts.

Finally, they emerged onto a quiet street. Ayaan paused, turning to face Zainab. The moonlight cast a gentle glow over them, creating a moment of serene beauty amidst the turmoil. He reached out, brushing a strand of hair from her face.

"Are you alright?" he asked softly, his eyes filled with concern.

Zainab nodded, feeling the warmth of his touch. "As long as I'm with you," she

whispered, her voice barely audible.

In that silent moment, the world around them seemed to disappear. Ayaan gently pulled her closer, wrapping his arms around her in a protective embrace. The fear and uncertainty melted away, leaving only the profound connection between them.

"Ayaan, promise me something," Zainab said, her voice trembling. "Promise me

that no matter what happens, we'll find a way to be together."

Ayaan's grip tightened, his heart aching with the weight of their circumstances. "I swear on every star ill stand by you ," he whispered, his voice choked with emotion. "I will never let go of you, Zainab."

Their foreheads touched, and time seemed to stand still. The intimacy of their closeness, the electricity between them, felt like a lifeline amidst the chaos. Ayaan's hand moved to the back of Zainab's neck, his fingers tangling gently in her hair. She closed her eyes, letting the sensation of his touch calm her racing heart.

"I love you, Zainab," Ayaan whispered, his voice breaking with sincerity.

Tears welled in Zainab's eyes as she whispered back, "And I love you, Ayaan."

The kiss that followed was soft and tender, a melding of two souls seeking

solace in each other. It was a promise of devotion, a vow to withstand the storm together. In that fleeting moment, nothing else mattered—the world could crumble around them, but their love would remain unshaken.

The night stretched on, filled with whispered confessions and lingering touches. They knew the road ahead would be fraught with danger and uncertainty, but they also knew their love was strong enough to face it all. As they held each other under the moonlit sky, they felt an unbreakable bond that would guide them through the darkest of times.

In the weeks that followed, the political unrest intensified. Protests erupted in the streets, and violent clashes became a daily occurrence. Lahore, once a city of vibrant diversity, was now a battleground of fear and hatred. Zainab and Ayaan's stolen moments became even more precious as the world around them descended into chaos.

One evening, as they met in a secluded garden, Ayaan's eyes were dark with worry. "I've heard rumors," he said quietly, taking Zainab's hand in his. "They're planning mass evacuations. People are being forced to leave their homes."

Zainab's heart clenched with fear. "What will happen to us?" she whispered, her voice trembling.

Ayaan pulled her into his arms, holding her tightly. "We will find a way," he promised. "No matter what, we will be together."

As the sun set, casting a golden hue over the garden, they sat together in silence, drawing strength from each other's presence. The world outside was changing, but in that moment, their love felt timeless and unbreakable.

The next day, Ayaan surprised Zainab with a delicate necklace, a single pearl hanging from a thin chain. "For you," he said, placing it around her neck. "A symbol of our love, something to hold onto when we are apart."

Zainab touched the pearl, feeling a rush of emotion. "I will cherish it always," she said, her eyes filling with tears.

As days turned into weeks, their meetings became increasingly dangerous. The unrest in the city escalated, and the fear of discovery loomed over them like a dark cloud. Yet, each time they met, the world seemed to fade away, leaving only the intense connection between them.

One stormy night, as they sheltered in an abandoned house, the rain beating against the windows, Ayaan reached for Zainab's hand. "I want you to know,"

he said softly, "that you are my everything. No matter what happens, our love will endure."

Zainab's heart swelled with love and determination. "And you are mine," she replied, her voice steady despite the storm raging outside.

They held each other close, their hearts beating as one. The rain poured down, but inside, they were wrapped in the warmth of their love. No matter the challenges that lay ahead, they knew that their bond was unbreakable, a beacon of hope in a world torn apart by hatred and fear.

The next morning, as they parted ways, Zainab felt a pang of fear. "Be careful," she urged, her eyes searching his. "I can't bear the thought of losing you."

Ayaan pressed a kiss to her forehead. "I will, my love," he promised. "And we will be together again soon."

As Zainab watched him disappear into the crowd, she clutched the pearl necklace, a tangible reminder of their love. The uncertainty of the future loomed large, but she knew that as long as they had each other, they could face anything.

♡♡♡

THREE

SHIFTING SANDS

As the city of Lahore continued to fracture, so did the lives of those within it. The political unrest that once simmered now boiled over, turning the streets

into a battleground. Amid the chaos, Zainab and Ayaan's love story found both its greatest strength and its deepest challenges.

Zainab woke up to the sound of muffled cries and hurried footsteps. Her family gathered in hushed conversations, their faces etched with worry. Her father, usually stern and unyielding, now looked defeated. "We need to leave," he declared, his voice trembling. "The violence is spreading, and it's no longer safe here."

The words struck Zainab like a bolt of lightning. The fear of separation from Ayaan consumed her. As her family packed their belongings, Zainab found a moment to sneak out. She ran through the alleyways, her heart pounding with every step, until she reached the trinket stall.

Ayaan was already there, his face a mask of concern. "Zainab," whispered, pulling her into a tight embrace. "I've heard. My family is preparing to leave."

Tears streamed down Zainab's face. "I can't bear the thought of losing you," she cried. "What will we do?"

Ayaan cupped her face in his hands, his eyes filled with determination. "We will find a way," he promised. "No matter what, we will be together."

In that moment, they made a pact—a vow to stand by each other, come what may. The fear of the unknown loomed large, but their love was a beacon of hope in the darkness. They shared a tender kiss, a promise of devotion and resilience.

As the day's passed, the city descended further into chaos. Families were torn apart, homes reduced to rubble, and the streets ran red with blood. Zainab and Ayaan's stolen moments became even more precious, their love a refuge

amidst the turmoil.

Ayaan handed over the responsibility of his only family member left which is his grand mother to his friend Sameer and promised him he will be back soon as the political tension start to ease

One fateful day, as they met in a secluded spot by the river, Ayaan's face was grim. "There's no time left, Zainab said "My family might be leaving tonight in the darkness of hope ,Zainab's heart raced with fear and determination. "What should we do?"

Ayaan took her hand, his grip firm and reassuring. "We will meet at the old train station, at midnight. We will leave together, find a way to start a new life. Promise me you'll be there."

Zainab nodded, her eyes filled with resolve. "I promise," she whispered, her voice steady despite the fear gnawing at her heart.

As night fell, Zainab made her way to the old train station, her heart pounding with anticipation and dread. The station, usually bustling with life, now stood eerily silent, a ghostly reminder of the city's fractured past.

She waited, her breath catching with every sound, every shadow. And then, through the darkness, she saw him. Ayaan, his eyes alight with determination, running towards her. They embraced, their hearts beating as one.

"We will make it," Ayaan whispered, his voice a mix of hope and desperation. "Together, we will find our way."

As they boarded the train, leaving behind the only home they had ever known, they clung to each other, their love a guiding light in the uncertainty that lay ahead. The journey was fraught with danger, but as long as they were together, they knew they could face anything.

The train ride was long and arduous, filled with the cries of children, the hushed whispers of anxious families, and the somber silence of those who had lost everything. Zainab and Ayaan held each other close, drawing strength from their love. They whispered words of comfort and hope, their bond unbreakable.

As the train approached the border, tension filled the air. Armed guards patrolled the carriages, their eyes cold and unforgiving. Ayaan tightened his grip on Zainab's hand, his heart pounding with fear and determination. "Stay close," he whispered.

When the train finally stopped, the guards began to search the passengers, looking for anything suspicious. Zainab's heart raced as a guard approached them, his eyes narrowing. "Papers," he demanded.

Ayaan handed over their papers, his hands steady despite the fear gnawing at him. The guard scrutinized the documents, his expression unreadable. Satisfied with

Ayaan's papers, he turned to Zainab, his eyes narrowing with suspicion.

"These papers are not valid," the guard said coldly. "You must leave the train."

Panic surged through Zainab as she clutched Ayaan's hand tighter. "Please," she begged, her voice trembling. "There must be a mistake."

But the guard remained unmoved. "Off the train, now," he ordered. Ayaan's heart pounded with desperation. "She is with me," he pleaded. "We are together." The guard's expression remained stern. "The papers do not lie. She must leave." Tears streamed down Zainab's face as she looked at Ayaan. "What will we do?" she whispered, her voice breaking.

Ayaan's mind raced for a solution. "I'll come with you," he declared, stepping off the train with Zainab.The guard's eyes widened with surprise. "You are a fool,"

he said, shaking his head. "But do as you wish."

As the train pulled away, leaving them behind, Zainab and Ayaan stood in the cold night air, the reality of their situation sinking in. They were alone, stranded in a land filled with uncertainty and danger. But as they looked into each other's eyes, they felt a renewed sense of determination. "We will find a way," Ayaan said firmly, taking Zainab's hand. "No matter what, we will face this together."

In that moment, they made another vow—to stay by each other's side, to fight for their love, and to overcome any obstacle that stood in their way. The journey ahead would be difficult, but with their love as their guide, they knew they could endure anything.

As the morning sunlight pierced through the curtains, Zainab found herself standing in the exact same room that held her fondest memories. The walls that once echoed her laughter now reverberated with accusations. Her family's

anger and mistrust loomed large, as cold and unforgiving as the winter fog outside.

The promise made under the starry sky with Ayaan felt distant and unreachable, like a mirage that would vanish upon closer inspection. Her father's words,

harsh and unyielding, echoed in her mind. "You will not leave this house again," he had declared. Zainab's heart sank as she realized the enormity of the punishment. Her world had shrunk to the confines of her home, with the secret spot and the warmth of Ayaan's company now out of reach.

The narrative that once brimmed with promise and the thrill of clandestine meetings now pivoted to one of silent suffering and resilience. Zainab vowed to herself that she would not let this suffocating cage snuff out her spirit. The promise to meet Ayaan and the memories of their stolen moments would be her beacon in this darkness

That evening, Zainab's family invited Farhan and his family over to finalize the engagement. As the realization of what was happening dawned on her, Zainab felt her world shatter. Unable to process the betrayal and the overwhelming

sorrow, she retreated to her room, her heart breaking into pieces. She sobbed uncontrollably, the weight of her family's decision pressing down on her.

That evening, as the sun dipped below the horizon, casting a crimson glow over the city, Zainab's family handed her a red Muslim dress. The fabric shimmered with an almost mocking vibrancy, a stark contrast to the darkness that now clouded her heart. They instructed her to wear it for the engagement with Farhan's family.

As Zainab held the dress, tears welled up in her eyes. This dress, once a symbol of joy and celebration, now felt like a shroud of despair. She had envisioned wearing such a dress on her wedding day with Ayaan, not for an unwanted engagement. Every thread of the fabric seemed to weave a tale of lost dreams and unfulfilled promises.

The soft tinkling of the bangles that accompanied the dress—a sound she once cherished—now felt like the clanging of chains. Each chime echoed her heartache, amplifying the pain of the separation from Ayaan. The once-beloved melody of chudiyaan, which had filled her with anticipation and joy, now

became a cruel reminder of the shattered future she had dreamed with Ayaan.

As she reluctantly put on the dress, each movement was weighed down by sorrow. The mirror reflected not a bride-to-be but a prisoner of circumstances, trapped by the very traditions she had once held dear. The vibrant red, a color of love and passion, now mirrored the bleeding wounds of her heart.

Zainab's anguish deepened as she thought of Ayaan. The memories of their whispered promises and stolen glances played in her mind like a cruel film. She

clutched the pearl necklace Ayaan had given her, seeking solace in its delicate presence. Her heart cried out for him, every beat a silent plea for rescue.

In a final act of defiance, Zainab poured her grief into the letter she wrote to Ayaan. Through tear-stained pages, she expressed her despair and the unbearable weight of her family's decision. she wrote about the impending engagement and her anguish. She begged for his understanding and vowed that their love would withstand even this trial. Her hands trembled as she sealed the envelope, knowing it carried her heart's deepest sorrows and unwavering love.She handed the letter to her trusted friend, her eyes pleading for understanding. "Please, deliver this to Ayaan," she whispered, her voice choked with emotion. Her friend nodded, taking the precious missive and promising to ensure it reached him.

As Zainab watched her friend disappear into the night, she felt an

overwhelming sense of helplessness. The dress clung to her like a second skin, a constant reminder of the path her family had chosen for her. The future seemed bleak, but within her heart, the flame of her love for Ayaan continued to burn, a beacon of hope amidst the engulfing darkness.

That evening, the atmosphere in Zainab's home was heavy with anticipation and underlying tension. Her family members gathered, their faces solemn yet determined, as Farhan and his family arrived. The living room, usually filled with laughter and warmth, now felt like a cold, unforgiving chamber.

As the clock struck the hour, Zainab's father cleared his throat and announced, "We have set the wedding date for the 4th of February, two weeks from today."

The words echoed in Zainab's mind, each syllable like a nail sealing her fate. She felt a chill run down her spine, her heart pounding in her chest. The room seemed to close in on her, suffocating her with the weight of impending doom.

Farhan approached her, a smug smile playing on his lips. He took her hand, the touch cold and unfeeling. Zainab's eyes met his, and in that moment, she saw no trace of the compassion and understanding she so deeply craved. Farhan was a stranger, an intruder in her life and dreams.

As he slid the engagement ring onto her finger, Zainab felt her heart shatter into a thousand pieces. Tears welled up in her eyes, spilling over as she struggled to maintain her composure. Each tear was a silent scream, a desperate cry for the love she was being forced to abandon.

The family members around her clapped and congratulated the couple, their faces filled with pride and satisfaction. But for Zainab, the world had come crashing down. The sparkle of the ring on her finger was a cruel reminder of the dreams she had woven with Ayaan, now torn to shreds.

In that moment, Zainab realized that her life, once filled with the promise of love and happiness, had now become a series of compromises. The concept of joy had morphed into mere survival, a constant battle against the suffocating expectations and pressures of her family.

Her brother, standing beside her, whispered, "This is for the best, Zainab. Don't fight it." But his words felt hollow, an empty consolation for the profound loss she was enduring.

As the evening wore on, Zainab's mind drifted to Ayaan. She clutched the pearl necklace hidden beneath her dress, drawing strength from its presence. Her heart ached with the memory of their promises, their shared moments of tenderness and love. She knew that, despite the overwhelming odds, their bond remained unbroken.

Zainab's tears continued to flow as she stood beside Farhan, a symbol of her family's victory over her desires. But within her, a fire burned—a fire of love and defiance, a refusal to let go of the one person who truly understood and cherished her.

As the night drew to a close, Zainab resolved to hold onto that fire, to keep her love for Ayaan alive in her heart. No matter what fate had in store, she knew that their connection was stronger than any ring or forced engagement. And with that thought, she faced the uncertain future with a renewed sense of determination.

Days passed in a haze of sorrow for Zainab. Her tears had dried, leaving behind a hollow emptiness. One afternoon, as she sat in her room, clutching the pearl necklace, her friend Ayesha came rushing in, her face flushed with urgency.

"Zainab, a letter from Ayaan," she whispered, handing over the envelope with trembling hands.

Zainab's heart skipped a beat. With trembling fingers, she tore open the letter. Ayaan's familiar handwriting greeted her, each word brimming with emotion and despair.

"Zainab, my love,

I cannot find the words to express the torment I feel knowing you are being forced into this engagement. It feels as though my world has crumbled, and I am powerless to stop it. My heart breaks for you, and I can barely breathe without you by my side.

I cannot bear the thought of losing you to Farhan. The pain

is unbearable, and it haunts me day and night. But we must be strong, my love. We must find a way to be together.

Meet me at our secret spot this Friday. Sameer and I will be there, waiting for you. Ayesha will help you get there. We will face this together, and we will find a way to escape this nightmare.

I love you with all my heart, forever and always. Ayaan"

Zainab's tears flowed freely as she read Ayaan's words. The pain in his letter mirrored her own anguish, and she sobbed uncontrollably, feeling the weight of their separation more acutely than ever before. But amidst the sorrow, a glimmer of hope flickered in her heart. The promise of seeing Ayaan again, of finding a way to be together, gave her the strength to carry on.

The memories of their past moments together flooded her mind—their whispered conversations, their tender embraces, and the stolen kisses under the moonlit sky. Each memory was a precious gem, a testament to the love they shared.

As Friday approached, Zainab's heart raced with a mixture of anticipation and fear. She could barely sleep, her mind consumed with thoughts of Ayaan and their secret meeting. The fear of being caught, the dread of what her family might do if they found out, loomed large. But the thought of Ayaan's arms around her, of escaping the suffocating confines of her current life, kept her going.

The day arrived, and with Ayesha's help, Zainab slipped out of her house, her heart pounding with every step. They made their way to the secret spot where she had shared so many precious moments with Ayaan. The air was thick with tension, but as they approached, Zainab's heart lifted at the sight of Ayaan and Sameer waiting for them.

Ayaan's face lit up with relief and joy as he saw her. He rushed forward, pulling her into a tight embrace. "Zainab," he whispered, his voice choked with emotion. "We will make it, I promise."

Sameer and Ayesha stood by, their faces filled with determination and support. "We will face this together," Sameer said firmly. "You two deserve to be happy."

As they stood there, surrounded by the echoes of their past and the promises of their future, Zainab felt a renewed sense of hope. The fear and uncertainty

still lingered, but with Ayaan by her side, she knew they could overcome any obstacle.

The group gathered in a hushed circle, their faces alight with determination and hope. They decided that Zainab and Ayaan would get married in secret on Sunday. The plan was set everyone would meet at Ayaan's house, where the ceremony would take place quietly.

Ayesha would bring the wedding dress for Zainab to ensure she wouldn't be seen leaving her house. The plan was meticulous, each detail crafted to ensure their union would be successful. The atmosphere was electric, filled with a mix of anxiety and excitement.

Zainab and Ayaan exchanged glances, their eyes shimmering with a blend of joy and sorrow. They embraced tightly, tears streaming down their faces. The hug was a mixture of relief and desperation, a silent promise to never let go. Zainab felt the strength of Ayaan's arms around her, and it gave her the courage she needed to face the days ahead.

As Zainab returned home, her heart was a whirlwind of emotions. In the one day that remained, she reminisced about every cherished moment they had shared. She remembered how they first met, the stolen glances, the secret meetings, and the love that had grown between them. The thought of finally being with Ayaan forever filled her with both hope and a bittersweet sadness. The fear of what lay ahead loomed over her, but the dream of a future with Ayaan kept her spirit buoyant.

Zainab clung to these memories, knowing that soon, their love would overcome all the barriers that had been placed in their path. With a heart full of anticipation and trepidation, she prepared for the day that would finally unite

her with Ayaan.

That Sunday, Zainab managed to concoct an excuse to leave the house, saying she needed to buy some items for the wedding preparations and that she would go with

Ayesha. Hearing this, her family, thinking she was now willingly preparing for her marriage to Farhan, allowed her to leave. They were pleased, assuming she had accepted her fate.

Zainab arrived at Ayaan's house early, her heart pounding with anticipation and fear. As she stepped inside, she found only Ayaan's elderly grandmother at home. Ayaan had told her about his dadi, who was frail and mostly bedridden, with no one else to care for her but him.

In a faint voice, mistaking Zainab for Ayaan, his dadi called out, "Beta, where were you since yesterday? Why didn't you come home? Please give me some water. I was waiting for you."

Zainab's heart ached as she realized Ayaan hadn't been home since the previous day. She thought he must be busy with wedding preparations. She gently replied, "Dadi, it's me, Zainab, your daughter-in-law," and tears welled up in her eyes. She knelt beside the old lady, who was the only family Ayaan had, and promised, "I am here now, Dadi. I will take care of you from now on."

Zainab helped her drink some water, feeling a deep sense of responsibility. She decided to prepare something in the kitchen while waiting, imagining herself as

perhaps the first bride to cook for her own wedding feast. But she found nothing in the house to cook with. Ayaan's dadi, chuckled softly and said, "So, you are Ayaan's bride."

Zainab laughed through her tears and replied, "No, Dadi, I am your daughter- in-law.

Zainab waited, her heart fluttering with happiness as she thought about how

her dreams were about to come true. She reminisced every promise Ayaan had made to her and smiled, realizing she had never felt this happy in her entire life. The anticipation of being united with Ayaan filled her with joy, and she lost herself in thoughts of their love.

She imagined herself in the red wedding dress, the fragrance of roses surrounding her, everything seemed like a dream she was about to achieve. Zainab whispered to herself with a smile, "Ayaan, my love, today you will be mine forever."

As she waited, she couldn't help but recall every precious memory. The first time they met, the secret glances, the stolen kisses. Her heart swelled with each recollection. She pictured herself, radiant in her bridal attire, walking towards Ayaan, the love of her life. The roses she imagined surrounding her seemed to fill the air with a heady scent, intoxicating her with the promise of their future.

The hours slipped by unnoticed. The golden hues of the afternoon slowly faded into the soft blues of the evening. Zainab, lost in her dreams, didn't realize how much time had passed. Her heart raced with the thought of finally being

Ayaan's bride, of their love story reaching its beautiful culmination.

But as dusk settled, an uneasy feeling began to creep into her heart. She

glanced at the clock, her brow furrowing in concern. "Why hasn't Ayesha arrived yet? Where is everyone?" she thought, the first seeds of worry planting themselves in her mind. The romantic reverie she'd been lost in began to waver.

The silence around her grew louder, pressing in on her. The once comforting thoughts of Ayaan and their love now felt fragile, easily shattered by the encroaching fear. She remembered Ayaan's promises, his tender words, and clung to them desperately, trying to push back the rising tide of anxiety.

As the minutes turned into hours, the stillness of the night became suffocating. "Something must be wrong," Zainab thought, her heart pounding in her chest. The anticipation that had once filled her with joy now twisted into a knot of dread. She tried to shake off the fear, but it clung to her, growing stronger with each passing moment.

Remembering that Ayaan's dadi must be hungry, Zainab decided to step out and get some food for her. "Dadi, I'll get something for you to eat," she said softly, her voice trembling. She left the house, her mind racing with questions.

As she stepped onto the streets, a shiver ran down her spine. The city was eerily quiet, a stark contrast to the usual bustling activity. The stillness was unsettling, a silent reminder that something was amiss.

Fear gripped her heart as she wondered why the city felt so deserted. "Where is everyone? Why hasn't anyone come yet?" she thought, panic rising within her. The romantic daydreams she had just hours ago now seemed distant and fragile. The fear of the unknown began to overshadow her thoughts of love and happiness. As she hurried back to the house with some food, her mind was a whirlwind of worries. She couldn't shake the feeling that something was terribly wrong. The once bright and hopeful day had turned into a scene of eerie stillness and growing dread. And that bride who once sat with her dreams beautifully adorned is now waiting in anticipation for his loved onces

That Friday night when everyone gathered and decided together that they would hold the wedding at Ayaan's house on Sunday when zainab went back to his home. Ayaan,

Sameer, and Ayesha each returning to their homes, their hearts filled with hope and excitement for the upcoming secret wedding. They had meticulously planned every detail, believing that their love and determination would see them through.

But fate had other plans. As Ayaan and Sameer made their way towards home, The night was heavy with silence, yet beneath it lay an electric hum of hope, of

a love that had defied everything that had tried to tear it apart. Ayaan could still hear her soft laughter from just hours before, like delicate chimes cutting through the stillness. He was on his way to her, carrying nothing but the memory of her face, the promises they had whispered under moonlit skies, and

a simple band of gold that had once been his grandmother's—a symbol of their union, of their defiance against a world in turmoil.

But the road was lonely. Shadows lurked in the corners, voices whispering of anger, of hatred too dark for love to survive. The faces that emerged from the darkness bore anger and intent, strangers whose eyes reflected a fire that no plea could extinguish.

Ayaan tried to run, clutching the ring, but fate had other plans. He stumbled, and the world began to blur around him as he fell to the ground

Sameer, his closest friend, a gasp catching in his throat as he took in the scene. He dropped beside Ayaan, his own heart splintering at the sight of his friend broken, struggling to hold on to life by threads that seemed to be slipping from his grasp.

Ayaan's hand reached out, weak and shaking, as he tried to find Sameer's. He managed a faint, pained smile, his eyes shining with unshed tears, with dreams unfulfilled and promises unkept.

"Sameer... tell her..." he whispered, his voice thin as though every word cost him a lifetime. "Tell Zainab... I loved her with every breath... and ***I'll wait. In a world*** where no one can tear us apart."

Sameer felt his own heart shatter, his hand squeezing Ayaan's desperately, as though the strength of his grip alone could pull his friend back from the edge. He wanted to scream, to tear apart the very fabric of fate that had led them to this tragic ending. But instead, he could only watch as Ayaan's eyes, filled with pain and something softer, something eternal, slowly dulled, the light slipping away.

Tears slid down Sameer's cheeks, mixing with the blood on his hands as he held

his friend, feeling the cold creep into Ayaan's skin.

Ayaan's In his mind's eye, he saw Zainab—her eyes brimming with dreams, her smile soft and warm. He imagined her waiting, eyes scanning the horizon for him, her heart filled with the hope of a future together. He could feel the weight

of her love, as real as the ground beneath him, anchoring him even as the world around him grew dimmer.

And as his breaths grew shallow, he whispered her name, as if it were a prayer. "Zainab," he murmured, his voice weak yet filled with love. ***"Perhaps... in another world... in another life... I'll find you.*** And ***we'll dance in the rain as we decided... no shadows, no walls... just us."***

The pain began to fade, replaced by a strange calm, almost like the quiet that comes just before dawn. He held onto that image of her—a bride dressed in

the finest red, a smile as bright as the stars—as he drifted into a darkness softer than sleep, a place where he hoped she would someday find him.

And in the distant echoes of his fading heartbeat, it was as if he heard her voice, calling him back to a world that would never be, a world where their love could live free

The silence was shattered by a deafening gunshot, echoing through the night like the final note of a tragedy. Sameer staggered, feeling an icy, spreading pain blossom within him as he touched his chest and saw his own blood begin to stain his trembling hands. His vision blurred, and a helpless tear slipped from his eyes as he felt his strength drain away, his body succumbing to the unforgiving weight of fate.

He sank down beside Ayaan, their hands falling close, almost as if they were reaching out to each other one last time. Sameer's gaze softened as his eyes began to close, and in his final breaths, he remembered the message he had

vowed to deliver. Ayaan's words echoed in his mind, a promise of love that transcended life itself. ***"Tell her... that in another world, I'll be waiting."***

But now, that promise would remain unspoken. The message that could have carried Zainab through the darkness would never reach her; it would slip away, lost in the chaos of a world torn apart. The dreams, the hopes, the laughter of two friends—everything was silenced in that single, brutal moment.

And so, there in the dust and blood, the story of two friends came to a tragic end, swallowed by the sorrow of a land divided. The memories of those who had loved fiercely and lost everything would remain etched into the souls of those who survived, a wound that time itself would fail to heal. People would remember the pain, the losses that left entire families broken, the love stories and friendships that never saw their happy endings., a scar that still aches and reminds those who remember that some losses are too profound to be forgotten.

Ayesha steps out that fateful Sunday morning, her heart a tender symphony of love and longing, clutching Zainab's wedding dress—a crimson masterpiece, a fabric alive with the dreams of friendship and devotion. It was not just a dress to her but a piece of her soul she wished to give to Zainab, a promise of love, a prayer wrapped in silk and threads of gold. She could already picture Zainab's radiant smile, that quiet sparkle in her friend's eyes, as if the universe itself

would pause for a moment to revel in their happiness.

But as Ayesha walks through the winding streets, fate sharpens its cruel claws. A group of men appears, their eyes filled with the bitterness of old wounds, scarred by the divides of partition—a hatred that neither time nor mercy had healed. Ayesha tries to look past them, clutching Zainab's dress tighter to her chest, willing her heart to be strong. She tries to walk faster, silently praying to reach Zainab, but the men encircle her, their anger simmering, twisting into a terrible storm.

Their taunts grow sharper, their jeers like splinters that pierce her fragile heart. But Ayesha's spirit, as delicate as it is, refuses to shatter—until they seize her. Ayesha, trembling yet resolute, is rendered helpless, her voice breaking like glass, as she realizes escape is slipping from her grasp. The precious dress— once vibrant with hope and life—is torn from her arms, dragged into the violence and shadows.

In their rage, they set her ablaze, as though her dreams and her kindness could somehow silence their fury. Flames consume the crimson silk, the wedding dress now soaked in her blood, a macabre blend of red that was never meant to be. Her world spins as the heat intensifies, yet her mind drifts far away, to a gentle vision of Zainab waiting with hopeful eyes, waiting for her love, her life, and for

a friend who will never come.

In those last moments, as her fragile spirit fades, Ayesha's heart breaks, not for herself but for the future she'll never witness. Her dreams scatter like ashes on the wind, her soul slipping away with Zainab's name on her lips, carrying the shadow of unfulfilled promises into eternity. She closes her eyes one last time,

imagining Zainab's smile—a glimmer of joy that will never know of the love that died with Ayesha that day.

Zainab stood at Ayaan's door, her heart filled with hope and love, waiting for him to return. She was unaware of the cruel fate that had befallen Ayaan, Ayesha, and Sameer. The silence of the empty house echoed her anxious breaths. She clutched a letter Ayaan had written to her, promising they would be together forever. With every passing moment, the sun dipped lower, casting long shadows that whispered the truth she couldn't hear: her beloved Ayaan had made a promise to meet her in a different world.

As the stars began to dot the sky, Zainab's anticipation turned into desperation. She paced the floor, glancing out the window every few seconds, whispering prayers and making silent vows. Her heart broke a little more with every passing hour. Tears streaked down her face, her breath hitched in sobs, but she held onto hope, refusing to let go.

She had no one to tell her that Ayaan, her love, was gone forever. She was stranded in a painful limbo, waiting for someone who would never come back. The night seemed endless, each second an eternity of heartbreak. The weight of unknowing love and lost promises crushed her spirit, but she waited still, because hope was all she had left. She couldn't fathom that her love had been taken to a world where she couldn't follow. The scene was a blend of sorrow, love, and a heartbreaking truth that no words could truly convey.

The next morning found Zainab sitting by the door, eyes red, and soul weary, still waiting for Ayaan. The weight of despair settled deep within her, but she

remained, forever waiting for a love that had promised to meet her in another realm.

Zainab, her eyes swollen from crying, moves through the kitchen like a shadow, every clink of the teacup a reminder of Ayaan. She prepares the chai for

Ayaan's grandmother with hands that tremble, imagining Ayaan's voice telling

her it'll be okay.

Despite everything, she holds onto the impossible hope that Ayaan will return. She wanders to the riverbank where they used to meet, the place filled with their laughter and stolen kisses. The river flows on, mocking her stillness, the world moving while her heart remains anchored in the past.

Sitting at their favorite spot, Zainab's sobs merge with the murmur of the water. "Where are you, Ayaan? Why haven't you come back?" she cries, her voice breaking. She remembers their plans, the dreams they had woven together. It's as if she feels his touch, his presence so real it's almost painful.

Being there, surrounded by memories, she feels Ayaan beside her, his head gently resting on her shoulder, his breath warm against her skin. "I'm broken without you," she whispers. Ayaan's voice, sweet and soft, seems to reach her ears, "We'll meet again, Zainab. Just like we promised. Away from everyone, under the rain, just us."

The imagined moments are so vivid, so tender, that she almost believes he's there. She can see his smile, feel his heartbeat against hers. "We'll be together," she says to the empty air, her tears mingling with the raindrops that start to fall.

She feels the rain soaking through her clothes, just like they had always dreamed.

The world around her fades, leaving just her and the memory of Ayaan, holding onto the love that transcends even death. It's a moment of pure, aching beauty—one that speaks of a love that is eternal, unbroken by the bounds of

life and death.

Zainab sat by the riverbank, tears flowing as she clung to the hope that Ayaan would return. She remembered his promise: "Jab tak aasman me sitare rahenge, mai tumse pyar karta rahunga, Zainab." The memory of his words gave her strength, even as her heart broke a little more each day.

The river, a silent witness to their love, seemed to carry echoes of their laughter. She sat there, lost in the past, crying her heart out. Suddenly, she felt a gentle hand on her shoulder. Her heart skipped a beat, believing Ayaan had come back. But as she turned around, she saw her brother standing there, concern etched on his face. Her family, who had been searching for her for two days,

was with him.

They bombarded her with questions, their voices a blur. Zainab, a shadow of her former self, could barely respond. She had become a ghost of the woman she once was, her spirit broken. Her family, seeing her in such a state, gently led her back home, away from the river that held so many memories and so much pain.

The scene was heartbreaking, filled with the anguish of lost love and the faint glimmer of hope that refused to die.

As Zainab left the riverbank, she carried with her the weight of her grief and the memory of Ayaan, forever etched in her heart

Zainab, completely unresponsive to the world around her, seemed lost in a void. Her family buzzed around, busy with wedding preparations, but she felt nothing. Her world had already ended. The only thing that occupied her mind was the time she spent with Ayaan. She clutched the necklace he had given her, the wooden box that held their memories, and the letter he had written, which she had read in the rain. These memories were her only solace, yet they

brought a flood of tears.

Each time she remembered Ayaan's smile, his touch, the sound of his voice, it was as if her heart shattered anew. She sat by the window, the rain tapping against the glass, mirroring the tears on her cheeks. She could almost feel Ayaan beside her, his presence so strong it felt real. She whispered into the emptiness, "Where are you, Ayaan? I'm broken without you."

The memories played like a film in her mind—their secret meetings by the river, the promises made under the stars, the stolen kisses, and shared dreams. She sobbed, her body wracked with the weight of her loss, feeling as though she

was drowning in her sorrow. The ache in her heart was unrelenting, a constant reminder of what she had lost.

Zainab's family watched in helplessness, seeing her transform into a shadow of

her former self. They knew the pain she was in but felt powerless to reach her

FOUR

DANCE OF DESTINY

The preparations for her wedding seemed almost cruel in the face of her anguish. They took her back home, hoping that familiar surroundings might bring her some peace, but Zainab remained adrift in her sea of heartbreak, clinging to the memories of a love that would never return.

The wedding day arrived, but it felt like a distant nightmare to Zainab. Her family dressed her in a beautiful red gown, but she was barely conscious of

what was happening around her. All she wanted was an answer: "Ayaan, tumne vada kiya tha ki tum aoge, kahan ho tum?" Her eyes had run dry of tears, leaving her in a numb haze.

As the preparations continued, a sudden hush fell over the house as news spread of an elderly woman's death. Amidst the chaos, Zainab caught fragments of the conversation, learning that the woman had died of starvation, having spent her life caring for others only to be abandoned in her final days.

The words hit Zainab like a punch in the gut. The woman was none other than Ayaan's grandmother, the very heartbeat of his memories. Her heart shattered all over again, and somehow, the tears she thought were gone started to flow anew.

In that moment, Zainab felt her entire world crumble. Her mind replayed all the moments with Ayaan—his laughter, his promises, his love. The weight of it all pressed down on her, crushing her spirit. She cried out silently, feeling as though the world around her had stopped, leaving her in a void of endless sorrow.

Her family, seeing her state, tried to console her, but Zainab was beyond reach. She was a fragile shell, haunted by the love that was stolen from her. The scene was a tragic symphony of heartbreak, woven with the threads of lost promises and the relentless ache of unfulfilled love. It was as if every tear and every cry echoed the depth of her pain, making the moment unbearably poignant.

A girl who once dreamed of her little world lost everything. Her love, her only friend—she lost everything to the ravages of partition. She witnessed the death of Ayaan's grandmother due to hunger, and countless others who succumbed during that time, their stories lost to history, never to be told.

Back then, so many dreamed of creating a small, peaceful world for themselves, but partition shattered everything. Zainab's story is not just her own but a reflection of thousands of untold stories, wrapped in silence.

Zainab's life revolved around a single dream, but when dreams shatter, all that remains is pain and solitude. This tale paints a picture of those moments of sorrow, which everyone keeps buried deep in their hearts but never speaks of.

It's a heart-wrenching story, but behind every story of pain lies the possibility of a new journey. One day, every broken dream will find a way to piece itself back together, in a new form, with renewed hope.

Zainab sat in the new, unfamiliar room on her wedding night. The weight of the red bridal dress felt like a heavy shroud, stifling her. She barely knew the man she was now married to, only that he drank heavily. The room's oppressive silence seemed to press down on her, and she felt as if the walls were closing in, trying to swallow her whole.

She wept silently, her tears hidden beneath the heavy bridal veil. No one was there to hear her cries, no one to offer comfort. Underneath that veil was a girl whose dreams had all been shattered. Zainab had hoped for so much, had believed in Ayaan's promises of love everlasting, "Jab tak aasman me sitare rahenge." Now, those promises were nothing but empty echoes in her mind.

Her thoughts drifted to Ayaan, to the love they had shared, the plans they had made. She remembered the necklace he had given her, the wooden box filled with their shared memories, the letter she had read in the rain, soaked in both water and her tears. These memories were all she had left, and they only deepened her sorrow.

As she sat there, her heart aching, she heard distant voices talking about an old woman who had died, abandoned by her children. The words struck her like a lightning bolt—Ayaan's grandmother. The pain of this new loss ripped through her, and fresh tears began to fall.

Zainab's heart shattered anew. She felt as though a part of her had died with Ayaan and his grandmother. She no longer had the strength to dream even her tears seemed to run dry. She was a bride in name only, her spirit broken, sitting alone in a room that felt more like a prison.

The scene was unbearably poignant, filled with the raw emotion of lost love and shattered dreams. Zainab's heartache was a silent scream, a fragile whisper of what once was, now lost to the cruel hands of fate. She sat there, waiting—not for a new beginning, but for an end to her suffering. It was a moment painted

in sorrow, tinged with the bittersweet memories of a love that transcended even death.

As Farhan about to stepped into the room, his heart was brimming with dreams and hopes. This was the moment he had fantasized about for so long—the moment he would see his bride for the first time. He had secretly bought a beautiful ring for Zainab, hiding it from his family, wanting to surprise her with a symbol of his love.

His mind was a whirlwind of thoughts and emotions. He imagined the look on Zainab's face when she saw the ring, the joy that would light up her eyes, the happiness that would fill their lives. Each step he took was filled with anticipation, his heart racing with excitement and a touch of nervousness.

As he approached, his mind painted vivid pictures of their future together. He saw them sharing laughter, building a life filled with love and understanding. Farhan's dreams were a beautiful tapestry of moments he wished to create with Zainab, each thread woven with care and affection.

The room, in its quiet simplicity, felt like a canvas ready to capture the essence of their love story. The shadows played their part, adding a romantic touch to the ambiance, as if the room itself was eager to witness the unfolding of a new chapter in their lives.

In Farhan's perspective, this moment was nothing short of magical. The air was thick with unspoken promises, dreams waiting to be realized, and a love that was eager to blossom. Every thought, every feeling was exaggerated in his heart, making this night an unforgettable chapter in their story.

As Farhan's eyes met Zainab's, and he offered a gentle salam, Assalamualaikum voice filled with warmth and respect.

Zainab, her heart trembling with a mix of fear and unexpected tenderness, responded in a soft, almost inaudible voice.

The world around them seemed to fade into an ethereal glow. Every shadow in the room became a canvas for their unspoken emotions, every breath a silent promise of love.

Farhan walked towards Zainab with a heart full of dreams. He held the delicate ring, hidden in his palm, a symbol of his undying love. As he got closer, he could see the mix of emotions in Zainab's eyes—fear, uncertainty, but also a glimmer of hope. His heart ached to erase her fears, to fill her life with joy.

In the dim light, Farhan took Zainab's hand gently, his touch soft yet firm, reassuring her of his presence. He whispered her name, his voice a tender melody that resonated with the love he held in his heart. He brought the ring out from his pocket, presenting it to her with a shy, yet confident smile.

Zainab's breath hitched as she saw the ring, a tear escaping her eye. Farhan, seeing her tears, felt an overwhelming urge to comfort her. He moved closer, his other hand softly wiping away the tear. "Zainab," he whispered, "This ring is a promise, a symbol of the life I dream for us. I want to build a future with you, filled with love and happiness."

The moment was beautifully surreal. The room, which once felt like a cage, now felt like a sanctuary of love. Every corner seemed to echo their silent vows, every shadow a witness to their budding romance. Farhan's heart swelled with love as he slipped the ring onto Zainab's finger, sealing his promise with a gentle kiss

on her hand.

As Farhan and Zainab exchanged soft, tentative words, the room seemed to hold its breath. Farhan, wanting to console her, gently took Zainab's hand and leaned in to kiss it. The moment his lips touched her skin, tears began to well up in Zainab's eyes. She tried to hold them back, but the dam broke, and she started to cry, her body trembling with the weight of her sorrow.

Seeing her in such pain, Farhan's heart ached. He felt a deep sadness wash over him, mirroring her emotions. He held her hand tighter, his voice soft and filled with concern. "Zainab, are you not happy with this marriage?" he asked, his own eyes glistening with unshed tears.

Zainab's sobs grew louder, her tears flowing freely now. The room, which had once felt like a sanctuary of new beginnings, now seemed to echo with the sound of her heartbreak. Farhan, who had entered the room with dreams of a beautiful future, felt his own heart breaking at the sight of her pain.

He moved closer, his other hand gently wiping away her tears. "Please, tell me what's wrong," he whispered, his voice trembling. "I want to understand, to help you."

Zainab, her voice choked with emotion, tried to speak but could only manage a few broken words. "I... I can't... It's too much," she cried, her body shaking with the force of her sobs.

Farhan's own tears began to fall as he listened to her. He felt a deep connection to her pain, a desire to take it all away and replace it with happiness. He wrapped his arms around her, holding her close, offering her the comfort of his embrace.

The room, once filled with dreams of a new life, now held the raw, unfiltered emotions of two souls trying to find their way. Farhan's heart ached for Zainab, and he vowed to be there for her, to help her heal and find happiness again.

The scene was a poignant blend of sorrow and tenderness, a testament to the fragile beauty of human emotions. It was a moment that would forever be etched in their hearts, a reminder of the power of love and the strength it takes to face the unknown together.

Farhan held Zainab tightly as she cried, her tears soaking into his shoulder. The weight of her sorrow felt unbearable, but he was determined to be her strength. "Please, Zainab, let me in," he whispered, his voice breaking. "I want to share your pain, to help you find a way through this."

Zainab's sobs gradually lessened, and she looked up at Farhan, her eyes red

and swollen. She saw the genuine concern and tenderness in his gaze, and for a moment, she felt a flicker of hope. "I'm... I'm just so lost," she admitted, her

voice barely audible. "Everything I loved is gone, and I don't know how to move

on. I don't know where he is, where all my friends are. I don't know why they left me."

"Farhan," she whispered her voice cracking , I loved Ayaan more than life itself, We had dreams, plan for a future that were stolen by someone . I am lost without him, I do not want to live .

Farhan gently squeezed her hand, his heart breaking for the pain she had endured. "Zainab, I can't change the past, but I promise you, I will be here for you. I will help you to heal.

Tears streamed down Zainab's face as she looked into Farhan's eyes, seeing the sincerity in them. The room, filled with shadows and whispers of the past, now felt like a space of new beginnings. Farhan's presence was a beacon of hope, a promise of a future that, while different, could still hold happiness.

In that tender moment, Farhan leaned in and kissed her hand once more, a gesture of comfort and reassurance. Zainab's tears continued to flow, but this time, they were mixed with a glimmer of hope. She felt a strange sense of peace, knowing that she was not alone in her grief.

The room, which had been a symbol of fear and sorrow, now began to transform into a sanctuary of healing and love. Farhan's gentle words and unwavering support began to soothe Zainab's broken heart. The night, which had started with so much dread, now held the promise of a new journey together.

Farhan, his own eyes glistening with tears, whispered, "We will get through this, Zainab. You are not alone anymore." His words, filled with love and compassion, wrapped around her like a warm embrace, slowly easing the pain that had consumed her.

Farhan's gentle embrace and heartfelt words started to calm Zainab's stormy emotions. Her tears, though still flowing, began to ease. Farhan looked into her eyes, his own filled with compassion and determination.

"Zainab," he whispered, his voice steady and soothing, "We'll find Ayaan together. We will search for him and your friends. You won't have to face this alone anymore."

Zainab's sobs softened as she absorbed his words. The promise of not being alone in her search, of having someone by her side, brought a new sense of hope. Farhan's eyes bore into hers with unwavering sincerity, making her believe that maybe, just maybe, there was still a chance for happiness.

Farhan held Zainab's hand firmly, his touch a silent vow of support and love.

"We will find them, Zainab," he reassured her "

The night, which had started with so much pain, now held a glimmer of hope. Farhan's promise to help her find Ayaan brought a new perspective, a possibility that the future could still be bright. The love and compassion in his eyes gave Zainab the strength she needed to face the unknown.

As the dawn began to break, the first light of a new day crept into the room, casting a soft glow on their intertwined hands. Zainab and Farhan, bound by their shared pain and newfound hope, It was a poignant moment of healing and love, the beginning of a new chapter in their lives.

As the wedding festivities wound down, Farhan stepped up in every possible way to support Zainab. His family welcomed her with open arms, showering her with the love and warmth she had longed for but never received from her own home. The house, filled with laughter and joy, contrasted sharply with the

sorrow Zainab carried in her heart.

In those early days, Zainab's worries about Farhan's drinking seemed like a distant concern. His kindness and unwavering support shone brightly, overshadowing any flaws. Farhan had a gentle way of being there for her, of knowing just when she needed a comforting word or a silent companion. His presence was like a soothing balm to her wounded soul.

The environment in Farhan's home was a stark contrast to what Zainab had known. She felt enveloped in a cocoon of love and acceptance, something she hadn't experienced before. Farhan's family treated her like one of their own, their affectionate gestures slowly mending the cracks in her heart. They understood her pain without prying, offering their support in silent, meaningful ways.

Farhan himself was a man of integrity and deep character. His one vice, drinking, was a small blemish on an otherwise commendable persona. He was attentive and caring, always putting Zainab's needs above his own. Farhan's strength lay in his ability to understand her without words, to be her silent support amidst the chaos of life.

During the wedding celebrations, Farhan remained by Zainab's side, guiding her through the festivities with gentle encouragement. He sensed her discomfort and made sure she never felt alone. In every dance, every ritual, Farhan's touch was light, yet reassuring, his smile a constant source of comfort.

Their home, filled with the joyful noise of family and friends, became a sanctuary of healing for Zainab. The love and care she found in Farhan and his family began to sew together the pieces of her broken heart. Every gesture of

kindness, every shared laugh, slowly built a bridge of trust and affection between her and Farhan.

Despite the whirlwind of wedding activities, Farhan's unwavering support did

not waver. He understood the depths of her grief and stood by her, offering his strength and love. His patience and compassion started to break down the walls Zainab had built around her heart, allowing her to see the possibility of a new beginning.

Farhan's presence, combined with the love from his family, began to restore Zainab's faith in life and love. The days were filled with a tender mix of joy and sorrow, the pain of the past blending with the hope for the future. And through it all, Farhan's quiet strength and gentle heart were the anchors that kept

Zainab grounded.

The partition tore through the heart of the subcontinent like a jagged knife, leaving behind a legacy of grief, pain, and division. India and Pakistan emerged as two separate entities, but the wound of separation bled deeply into the lives of millions. Lahore, once a thriving hub of culture and unity, now stood as a testament to the horrors of partition. The once-bustling streets were eerily silent, the air thick with the sorrow of those uprooted from their homes and lives.

Communities that had lived side by side for centuries were suddenly divided by a hastily drawn border. Neighbors became strangers overnight, and friends found themselves on opposite sides of a political chasm. The city of Lahore, now part of Pakistan, grappled with this new reality. Its once vibrant tapestry of Hindu, Muslim, and Sikh cultures was now a fragmented mosaic of loss and longing.

The aftermath was chaotic and tragic. Families were torn apart, with loved ones lost in the mass migration. Trains arrived at their destinations packed with people but stained with the blood of violence. Refugee camps sprang up, filled with souls haunted by the horrors they had witnessed. Lahore, which had once been a city of dreams, was now a city of broken hearts and shattered lives.

Yet, amidst the ruins, the indomitable spirit of the people began to stir. Lahore started to rebuild itself, piece by painful piece. The scars of partition were deep, but the resilience of its inhabitants was deeper. Slowly, markets reopened, schools welcomed students, and the sounds of everyday life began to return. The city that had been brought to its knees by division began to rise again.

Families that had stayed behind or newly settled found solace in each other. The streets started to fill with the aroma of food, the calls of vendors, and the

laughter of children—each sound a testament to the city's rebirth. The Gurdwaras, Mosques, and Temples, once symbols of a unified religious fabric, stood as reminders of what had been lost and as beacons of hope for a future where coexistence might once again flourish.

The city's architecture, marked by the grandeur of the Mughal era and the elegance of British colonial influence, stood resilient against the backdrop of a new, tumultuous era. Lahore's soul, though battered, was unbroken. Through the pain and loss, the city clung to its identity, its heritage, and its dream of once again becoming a place of harmony and cultural richness.

The journey to reclaim its former glory was fraught with challenges, but each step forward was a victory over the darkness of partition. Lahore's story was one of heartache and hope, a testament to the resilience of the human spirit and

the enduring power of love and community.

Farhan was not just any man he was a dedicated doctor who had devoted his life to healing others. His days were spent in the hospital, tending to the sick and injured, bringing comfort and hope to those in pain. He was known for his gentle bedside manner and his unwavering commitment to his patients.

Zainab, before their marriage, had no idea about this side of Farhan. She had heard only snippets about him, primarily focusing on his habit of drinking. It wasn't until after their wedding that she discovered the depth of Farhan's character and his noble profession.

It was one evening, not long after their wedding, that Zainab found herself standing outside Farhan's clinic, drawn by the murmurs of patients praising the doctor inside. Curious and slightly apprehensive, she stepped inside, only to find Farhan in his element, compassionately attending to a patient. The realization

hit her like a wave—this man, whom she barely knew, was a healer, a savior to many.

Farhan looked up and saw Zainab watching him. He gave her a small, reassuring smile, and in that moment, she saw him not just as her husband, but as a man dedicated to a higher purpose. The patients spoke of his kindness, his patience, and his skill, and Zainab's heart swelled with a newfound respect for him.

After finishing with his patients, Farhan walked over to her. "I wanted to tell you about my work," he said softly, "but I thought you needed time to settle first."

Zainab, her eyes filled with admiration and tears, nodded. "I had no idea," she whispered. "You're incredible."

Farhan took her hand gently. "I am just trying to make a difference," he said. "And now, with you by my side, I feel like I can do even more."

Their bond grew stronger as Zainab began to understand the depth of Farhan's

character. His profession as a doctor added a new layer to their relationship, one of mutual respect and admiration. Zainab started to accompany him to the clinic, learning more about his work and the lives he touched.

This revelation about Farhan's true self became a cornerstone of their marriage, showing Zainab that there was so much more to him than she had initially thought. It became clear that despite his one bad habit, Farhan was a man of integrity, compassion, and deep character.

One evening, Zainab sat by the window, lost in the memories that filled the wooden box Ayaan had gifted her. She held the letter tightly in her hands, tears streaming down her face as she read Ayaan's words over and over again. The letter spoke of Ayaan's deep love for her, how much he missed her when she wasn't around, and how he longed for the moments they spent together. He wrote about waiting for her at his shop, hoping to catch a glimpse of her, and

reminisced about the rainstorm where they got drenched together, laughing and holding each other close.

Zainab was so immersed in her memories and grief that she didn't hear Farhan enter the room. He stood silently behind her, watching the sorrow etched on her face. His heart ached for her pain, and he felt a deep sense of compassion and love for the woman he had vowed to support.

Quietly, Farhan stepped closer and read the letter over her shoulder. The words on the paper were a testament to a love so profound and pure that it touched his soul. He understood the depth of Zainab's loss and the weight of her grief.

Without a word, Farhan gently draped a blanket around Zainab's shoulders, his touch tender and reassuring. Zainab, startled, looked up and realized for the first time that Farhan was there. She saw the empathy and understanding in his eyes, and for a moment, her heart softened.

Farhan didn't say anything; he knew that words were insufficient in this moment. Instead, he gave her a small, comforting smile and quietly left the room, leaving Zainab alone with her memories and the warmth of his gesture.

The room felt different now, filled with the echoes of Ayaan's love and the gentle presence of Farhan's care. Zainab held the blanket tightly around herself, feeling a strange mix of sorrow and solace. Farhan's silent support was like a balm to her soul, offering her comfort without demanding anything in return.

The scene was beautifully poignant, a blend of heartbreak and hope. Farhan's quiet act of kindness spoke volumes, showing Zainab that she was not alone in her grief. It was a moment of connection, a delicate dance of emotions that hinted at the possibility of healing and new beginnings.

The next morning, sunlight filtered through the window, casting a gentle glow across the room. Zainab, still wrapped in the blanket Farhan had given her, looked out with a distant gaze, her mind heavy with memories and unspoken questions.

Farhan entered quietly, his heart aching at the sight of Zainab's sorrow. He walked over to her, his expression soft and determined. "Zainab," he said gently, "things are better now. We can start looking for your friends and Ayaan. Get ready; we'll go to the market today and ask around."

Zainab turned to him, her eyes wide with a mix of hope and uncertainty. The thought of finding answers, of finally understanding what had happened, stirred something deep within her. For the first time in a long while, she felt a spark of hope.

The mention of Ayaan's name brought a fresh wave of emotion. Tears welled up in her eyes as she struggled to find her voice. "Do you really think we'll find them?" she whispered, her voice trembling.

Farhan nodded, his eyes filled with determination and compassion. "Yes,

Zainab. We'll find them, and we'll find the answers you're looking for. You're not alone in this anymore."

The promise in Farhan's words wrapped around her like a lifeline. She felt the tears spill over, a mix of relief, sadness, and a glimmer of hope. Farhan reached out, gently wiping away her tears. "We'll do this together," he reassured her.

As Zainab readied herself, the room seemed to pulse with a new energy, the promise of a journey that could bring closure and healing. Farhan stood by her side, his presence a beacon of support and strength. He helped her gather her things, his touch gentle and comforting.

Together, they stepped out into the morning light, the market bustling with life and activity. Farhan held Zainab's hand, guiding her through the crowded streets. Every person they spoke to, every question they asked, felt like a step closer to the answers Zainab desperately sought.

With each inquiry, Zainab's heart raced, filled with anticipation and fear. The journey was fraught with emotion, the weight of the past mingling with the fragile hope of the present. Farhan's unwavering support gave her the strength to keep going, his presence a constant reminder that she was not alone.

The scene was a tapestry of raw emotion, woven with threads of sorrow, hope, and the enduring bond between two souls on a shared journey. Farhan's promise to Zainab became a beacon of light in their darkest hours, guiding them towards a future where the past could finally find its place.

Zainab and Farhan set out together, heading to the place where Zainab and Ayaan used to meet. As they arrived, the familiar fragrance of the spot enveloped Zainab, pulling her into a whirlwind of memories. Every scent, every sound reminded her of the times they had spent together, their secret rendezvous filled with love and laughter.

She felt the weight of nostalgia as she walked to the riverbank. The gentle sound of the flowing water, the soft rustling of leaves, all beckoned her into the past. Zainab could almost see Ayaan standing there, waiting for her with that same loving smile, their laughter echoing in the air. She moved to sit by the edge of the river, her eyes fixed on the setting sun, lost in the sea of her memories.

The golden hues of the twilight reflected on the water, casting a dreamlike glow around her. Zainab's heart ached with longing as she thought of Ayaan and their stolen moments by the river. She remembered how they used to sit by the water, watching the sunset together, sharing their dreams and hopes.

In the midst of her reverie, Farhan quietly sat down beside her. He placed a comforting hand on her shoulder, his presence a gentle anchor in her storm of emotions. "Zainab," he said softly, his voice filled with empathy, "we will find Ayaan. I'm certain that as long as there are stars in the sky, I'll be by your side."

Tears welled up in Zainab's eyes, spilling over as she heard Farhan's words. The promise of finding Ayaan, coupled with Farhan's unwavering support, brought a mixture of pain and hope. Farhan gently wiped her tears, his touch warm and reassuring.

"We'll search together," Farhan continued, his eyes never leaving hers. "We'll find the answers you seek. You are not alone in this journey."

Zainab leaned into him, drawing strength from his presence. The scene was a poignant blend of sorrow and hope, the promise of a future where answers might finally be found. The setting sun painted the sky with shades of pink and gold, mirroring the emotions that swirled within her heart.

In that moment, the riverbank became a sacred space, a place where past and present converged, filled with the echoes of lost love and the promise of new beginnings. Farhan's words wrapped around Zainab like a protective embrace, his love a beacon of hope in her darkest hour.

As the first stars appeared in the evening sky, Zainab felt a flicker of hope ignite within her. She held onto Farhan's promise, ready to face whatever lay ahead with him by her side. The journey was far from over, but together, they would navigate the path of healing and discovery.

Their story, interwoven with threads of love, loss, and resilience, continued to unfold, promising a future where broken hearts could find solace and dreams could be reborn.

A month had passed since Zainab and Farhan began their search for Ayaan, Sameer, and Ayesha. Each day was a blend of hope and despair as they spoke to countless people, following every lead with unwavering determination. Some days, they would hear promising news—someone had seen a man named Ayaan, or a woman resembling Ayesha. Their hearts would race with anticipation, only to be met with disappointment when they discovered it was someone else.

Despite the setbacks, they never gave up. The journey was filled with moments of hope, where they believed they were close to finding their loved ones, and moments of despair, where the weight of their quest seemed too much to bear. Yet, through it all, Farhan remained Zainab's rock, his presence a constant source of strength and comfort.

Zainab and Farhan sit at the bustling tea stall, sipping their chai to unwind. Nearby, a group of elderly men discuss the harrowing memories of the partition, their voices laced with sorrow. One man recounts a gruesome incident—witnessing a girl being set ablaze while clutching a wedding dress.

Zainab's heart races at the mention of the bridal outfit. She remembers Ayesha was supposed to bring her wedding dress that day. Her eyes lock with Farhan's, a silent understanding passing between them. They approach the man, dread clawing at their insides.

With trembling hands, Zainab pulls out Ayesha's photo from her purse, her voice barely a whisper as she asks if this was the girl. The man's eyes widen, recognition flooding his features. He confirms their worst fears, recounting the tragic scene in vivid detail.

Zainab's knees buckle under the weight of the revelation. Farhan catches her as she falls, her sobs echoing in the now quiet stall. The people around, sensing their profound pain, respectfully look away.

Farhan catches Zainab as she crumbles, her sobs echoing in the now muted tea stall. The people nearby, initially curious, turn away out of respect for their pain. Farhan, though shattered himself, gathers the strength to thank the man. Every word feels heavy, as if their shared sorrow binds them in that moment.

Through the fog of their grief, Farhan gently guides Zainab away from the stall. Each step feels like a monumental effort as they walk back towards their home, the weight of Ayesha's absence pressing down on them. The night air carries a chill, but it's nothing compared to the cold emptiness Zainab feels inside.

At home, they sit in silence, the ghost of Ayesha's presence haunting every corner. Farhan tries to console Zainab, but what words could possibly fill the

void left by such a loss? They cling to each other, finding solace in their shared grief, knowing that despite the darkness, they have each other to lean on.

As the days turn into weeks, Zainab and Farhan's existence becomes a delicate dance with grief. They try to hold on to their routines, hoping that normalcy might bring a semblance of peace. But each corner of their home, each fleeting shadow, is a reminder of the void Ayesha left behind.

One evening, Zainab sits by the window, lost in thought. In her hands, she holds the wedding dress Ayesha was meant to deliver. The soft fabric feels like a cruel joke now, a symbol of shattered dreams. Zainab's tears fall silently, mingling

with the delicate embroidery. Farhan watches from a distance, his heart aching with helplessness.

Zainab starts talking about Ayesha, her voice trembling yet determined. She speaks of her friend's laugh, her kindness, and the light she brought into their lives. Farhan joins in, sharing stories of Ayesha's vibrant spirit and the dreams they once held dear. Their words weave a tapestry of memories, a fragile but beautiful way to keep Ayesha's presence alive.

Slowly, these conversations become their solace. They laugh through their tears, reminiscing about the happy times. Though the pain is ever-present, they find moments of warmth in the shared memories. Farhan holds Zainab close, promising her that as long as they remember Ayesha, she will never truly be gone.

Their journey through grief is far from over, but step by step, they start to heal. It's a testament to their resilience and love, finding a way to honor Ayesha while forging a path forward, together.

As the days drift into one another, Farhan finds himself noticing Zainab in ways he never had before. The subtle touches that once passed unnoticed now send a shiver down his spine, each contact a reminder of the depth of their shared grief and an emerging tenderness.

One evening, Zainab reaches for his hand, and in that fleeting moment, Farhan feels his heart skip a beat. It's as if time stands still, and the world fades away, leaving just the two of them suspended in their own universe. Her touch, soft and comforting, anchors him in a way he never imagined possible.

Farhan starts to cherish the small things—like the mornings they spent at the tea stall, the warmth of their shared chai, and the comfort of her presence by his side. Every glance, every shared smile, carries a weight of unspoken emotions. He finds solace in the mundane, like the way Zainab prepares his

meals, her hands moving with a practiced grace. Her caring gestures, once taken for granted, now feel like precious gifts, each one deepening his affection for her.

Their trips to the hospital, though wrapped in sorrow, also become a poignant reminder of their bond. Zainab's unwavering support, her quiet strength, makes Farhan see her in a new light. They walk home together, the silence between them filled with unspoken promises and growing intimacy.

One evening, as they take a walk through the bustling market, Farhan finds himself stealing glances at Zainab. The way she moves, her gentle smile, her kindness in the face of their shared grief—it all tugs at his heartstrings. He realizes that amidst the pain, something beautiful is blossoming. His heart, once consumed by loss, now beats with a new rhythm, one that syncs with Zainab's.

Their moments together become more than just shared routines; they become cherished memories. The world around them, though still tinged with sadness, also holds a promise of hope. Farhan's feelings for Zainab grow stronger with each passing day, the connection between them deepening in the face of their shared journey. It's a fragile, yet profound, romance, built on the foundations of their shared past and the promise of a future together

As the weeks go by, Farhan starts to see Zainab in a new light. The grief that once clouded his heart begins to clear, revealing the depths of her love and compassion. He notices the small, tender gestures she makes, the way her hair falls gently around her face, the light in her eyes that never dims despite their sorrow.

One afternoon, as they sit in the living room, an old Bollywood song plays softly in the background. The lyrics speak of eternal love and undying devotion, mirroring Farhan's growing feelings.

"Bahut raat beeti chalo main sula dun , Pawan Chhede Sargam , Main Lori Suna Dun"

the singer croons, and Farhan finds himself lost in the melody. He gazes at

Zainab, her presence soothing his troubled soul.

Every detail of her becomes a source of fascination. The way she dresses, her graceful movements, even her laughter—it all feels new and intoxicating. Farhan realizes how much he cherishes her, how her strength and kindness have been the anchors keeping him steady.

Their moments together, once routine, now feel charged with a quiet romance. The simple act of sharing a cup of tea becomes an intimate ritual, her laughter a balm to his weary heart. He can't help but steal glances at her, his heart swelling with affection each time she catches his eye.

Farhan's perspective shifts. He starts to see Zainab not just as a partner in grief, but as someone who fills his world with light and hope. The old Hindi songs that play become the soundtrack to their evolving love story, each lyric a reminder

of the bond that grows stronger every day.

Their walks, their talks, the way she takes care of him—all of it deepens his love for her. Farhan finds himself dreaming of a future where their love blooms, where they find joy and laughter again. It's a slow, beautiful realization that amidst the shadows of their past, something profoundly beautiful is emerging.

One day, Zainab and Farhan find themselves wandering through the vibrant market, its lively atmosphere a stark contrast to the shadows of their grief. And then the rain begins to pour, and in no time, both Farhan and Zainab are drenched. As Zainab stands in the downpour, she seems to dissolve into the rain itself, shedding all the sorrows of her life. Witnessing this, Farhan feels a thrilling sensation in his heart. The rain not only soaks them, but it also washes away all the pain and sadness, creating a magical and romantic moment

Farhan, captivated by Zainab's transformation in the rain, walks closer. The rain, heavy and relentless, creates a cocoon around them, isolating them from the rest of the world. Zainab, feeling the weight of her past dissolve, opens her eyes to meet Farhan's. Her smile, radiant and genuine, is the most beautiful thing Farhan has ever seen. He extends his hand, and without a second thought, Zainab takes it. In that moment, the rain isn't just water; it's a cleansing force, a silent witness to the birth of something extraordinary.

As the city around them fades into the background, they dance, no music but the rhythm of their hearts and the symphony of raindrops. And in the embrace of the monsoon, they find their own piece of paradise.

As they stand in the market, the melody weaves through the air, adding magic to their moment.

"Sun saathiya, maahiya, barsa de ishqa ki boondein,"

the song lilts, each note wrapping around Farhan's heart.

Zainab's eyes glisten with unshed tears, her smile trembling but radiant. Farhan, overcome with emotion, gently lifts her hand to his lips, kissing the back of it softly.

"Yeh moh moh ke dhaage, teri ungliyon se ja uljhe,"

the lyrics flow, perfectly mirroring the intricate bond they share.

In that instant, their love story finds its rhythm, the old Bollywood songs becoming the soundtrack of their hearts. Despite the pain, despite the loss, they've discovered a profound connection, one that promises hope and healing in the days to come.

Farhan holds Zainab's hand a little tighter, he knows that despite the sorrow, despite the loss, they have found something beautiful in each other. Their Feelings, born from shared grief, is a testament to their resilience and the enduring power of connection. It's a scene filled with emotion, beautifully dramatized, and deeply romantic.

As time passes, Zainab begins to see Farhan in a new light. Initially, all she knew of him was that he had a habit of drinking, and this had painted a rather negative picture in her mind. However, as the days turn into weeks, she starts noticing the small acts of kindness and the underlying goodness in him. The rough edges begin to smooth out, and she sees a man with a heart full of care and love.

Farhan's drinking habit, as it turns out, isn't as frequent as Zainab feared. She realizes that he only resorts to it when something deeply troubles him. And even then, he never drinks at home. On those rare nights when he does drink, he sits outside, under the open sky, gazing at the moon. It's a silent vigil, a moment of solitude and reflection, and Zainab begins to see the depth of his struggles.

One evening, Zainab watches from the window as Farhan, lost in thought, sits on the terrace. The moonlight bathes him in a gentle glow, highlighting the softness in his features. She notices the way his eyes, usually filled with sorrow, now carry a glimmer of hope. The gentle sway of his hair in the night breeze, the way his shoulders rise and fall with each deep breath—all of it captivates her.

She finds herself drawn to him, not just as a companion in grief, but as a man who has quietly stood by her side. The melodies of old Bollywood songs play softly in the background, their lyrics weaving a tapestry of romance.

"Lag jaa gale,

ke phir yeh haseen raat ho na ho," the music whispers, capturing the essence of the moment.

Zainab steps onto the terrace, her presence pulling Farhan from his reverie. She sits beside him, their shoulders brushing. He turns to look at her, and in his

eyes, she sees a mix of vulnerability and tenderness. Farhan reaches out, his fingers lightly tracing the lines of her hand. The touch sends a shiver down her spine, a silent promise of something beautiful amidst the pain.

As they sit under the starlit sky, Zainab realizes that Farhan's kindness, his quiet strength, and his unwavering support have become her anchor. The moonlight, the music, and their shared silence create a moment so filled with emotion that it feels almost surreal. It's a scene steeped in romance, their bond deepening with each passing day, promising a future where love and hope intertwine.

One evening, Farhan sits outside, a drink in hand, staring up at the moon. The night is calm, yet inside him, a storm rages. The moonlight washes over him, casting long shadows and reflecting the turmoil within.

Zainab, noticing his absence from the room, steps outside. She finds him there, under the open sky, lost in his thoughts. Her heart aches seeing him like this, unknowing the burden he carries. With a deep breath, she walks towards him, her presence gentle yet firm.

"Farhan," she says softly, her voice cutting through the night. He looks up, eyes filled with a mix of sorrow and longing. She sits beside him, their shoulders brushing. Her hand finds his, squeezing gently. "Why do you drink?"

Farhan's gaze shifts back to the moon. "Sometimes... it's the only way to silence the noise," he admits, his voice barely above a whisper. Zainab listens, her heart

breaking for him. She knows that his pain is deep, but her love for him is deeper still.

The silence between them stretches, filled with unspoken words and shared grief. Zainab gently turns his face towards her, her eyes searching his. "You don't need this to find peace, Farhan. I'm here. We're in this together." Her words are a balm to his wounded soul, their sincerity piercing through his defenses.

He nods, a single tear escaping down his cheek. She wipes it away, her touch tender. In that moment, under the moonlit sky, surrounded by the echoes of a timeless melody, they find solace in each other. Farhan realizes that with Zainab by his side, he doesn't need the drink to drown his sorrows.

Farhan, his voice heavy with raw emotion, looks deep into Zainab's eyes. The moonlight casts a gentle glow over them, highlighting the intensity of the moment. "Zainab," he begins, his voice trembling, "you haven't lost your love yet, but I have. I know the unbearable agony of losing someone who means the world to you. That's why I drink... to drown the pain that feels like it's tearing me apart from the inside."

He takes a deep breath, his eyes glistening with unshed tears. "Every night, when I look at the moon, I see her face. She was my everything, my heart and soul. But fate, cruel as it is, took her away from me. The drink is my only escape from the memories that haunt me."

Zainab, her heart breaking for Farhan, gently places her hand on his. "You don't need this to find peace, Farhan. I'm here for you. We're in this together."

Farhan, his gaze unwavering, continues, "I don't want you to experience the same loss I did. I don't want you to lose your love the way I lost mine. The pain is too much to bear."

Zainab, her eyes filled with a mixture of sorrow and compassion, whispers, "You loved her deeply, didn't you?"

He nods, a single tear escaping down his cheek. "Yes, I did. Her name was Ayesha. She brought light into my darkest days, and her absence has left a void that nothing can fill. But seeing you, your strength, and your love, it gives me hope that maybe, just maybe, I can find peace too."

Farhan, his eyes reflecting the moon's glow, takes a deep breath, the weight of his revelation pressing down on him.

"Zainab," he says, his voice cracking, "her full name was Ayesha Kalal."

The moment the name escapes his lips, Zainab's world shatters. She gasps, tears welling up in her eyes. "Ayesha Kalal?" she whispers, her voice trembling. "She was my best friend... the Ayesha we've been searching for."

The reality hits them both like a tidal wave. Zainab's tears flow freely, her sobs echoing in the silent night. "That day at the tea shop, the photo I showed... it was her," she cries, her voice breaking. The weight of their combined grief seems insurmountable.

Farhan's heart aches, seeing Zainab in such pain. His own eyes glisten with tears as he pulls her close, their shared sorrow binding them together. "Yes," he whispers, his voice filled with anguish. "It was her. It was Ayesha."

The night wraps them in its cold embrace as they hold each other, their tears mingling with the night air.

They sit together, the weight of their loss pressing down on them. Zainab's sobs gradually quiet, and she clings to Farhan, finding a fragile sense of comfort in

his presence. Their shared grief, while overwhelming, also strengthens their bond, creating a connection forged in the depths of their sorrow.

Under the soft glow of the moon, Zainab, still grappling with the revelation, looks into Farhan's eyes. "Farhan," she says, her voice gentle yet inquisitive, "if you don't mind, can I ask you something?"

Farhan nods, his gaze steady. "Of course, Zainab."

She takes a deep breath, her heart pounding. "Why didn't you marry Ayesha? And why did you say yes to marrying me if you both loved each other so deeply? Why did Ayesha never tell me?"

Farhan's eyes cloud with a mixture of sorrow and resignation. "Zainab," he begins, his voice heavy with emotion, "Ayesha and I knew from the very beginning that we could never be together. When I first met her, it was like a dream. The closer I got to her, the more we both realized that our love was impossible."

He pauses, letting the weight of his words sink in. "Did you ever notice Ayesha's surname? Kalal. She came from a family of Kalals, a lower Muslim caste known for making liquor. In our society, such divisions can be insurmountable. We knew that no matter how much we loved each other, our families and society would never accept us."

Zainab's eyes widen, her tears flowing freely. "Ayesha... she never told me. Why didn't she share this with me?"

Farhan sighs, a tear escaping down his cheek. "She didn't want you to carry the burden of our pain. She loved you too much to let you see her suffer. That day at the tea shop, when you showed the photo, it broke my heart to recognize her. I couldn't bring myself to tell you then because I didn't want to add to your grief."

Zainab, overwhelmed by the revelation, clutches Farhan's hand tightly.

They sit together in silence, the truth hanging between them like a fragile thread. The moon watches over them, a silent witness to their shared sorrow and the unspoken love that binds them. In that instant, Zainab sees Farhan in a new light—not just as a man who loved her friend, but as someone who has

been through his own battles, carrying the weight of a love that was never meant to be.

Farhan, his eyes filled with sorrow, looks deeply into Zainab's eyes. "You see, Zainab, in our faith, any form of intoxication is considered haram—completely forbidden. Ayesha's family, however, was deeply involved in the liquor business. It was their livelihood, a trade passed down through generations. My family, devout in their beliefs, could never accept this. I tried to make them understand, but it was all in vain."

Zainab listens, her heart aching for the love that was never allowed to flourish. Farhan continues, "Despite our love, the societal and religious barriers were too great to overcome. I couldn't convince my family, and Ayesha didn't want to

put you through the pain of knowing."

Zainab sat across from Farhan, her eyes wide with curiosity. "So, **how did you meet Ayesha?**" she asked.

ᑭᑭᑭ

FIVE

SHADOW OF YESTERDAY

" Farhan is telling Zainab the story how he met Ayesha ".

Farhan leaned back, his gaze distant, as if replaying a vivid memory. "It was a monsoon evening. The rain poured relentlessly, creating a symphony on the rooftops. I took shelter at a small chai ki dukan, and that's where I saw her for the first time. She was sitting quietly, absorbed in a plate of jalebi, her presence almost magical. At that moment, I could almost hear the words... ***Tere vaste***

mera ishq sufiyana, mera ishq sufiyana...'It felt as if the rain itself was singing for

her, drawing me into that moment."

"Sounds like fate," Zainab said, smiling.

"It felt like it," Farhan continued. "She loved jalebi – the way she savored each bite was like an art form. She ate with such passion, such shiddat, as if the world around her didn't exist. Here I was, a doctor, always conscious about health, yet watching her enjoy those jalebis made me forget all sense of logic. After that day, I started finding myself at that same chai ki dukan, hoping to see her again."

Zainab chuckled softly, "So, the health-conscious doctor was drawn to a girl who loved jalebis?"

"Yes," Farhan replied with a faint smile. "That monsoon meeting sparked something in me. Every time I returned to that chai ki dukan, it was just to catch a glimpse of her, to see her relish those jalebis with such intensity. It was strange, but those small moments became the highlight of my days. I simply wanted to be near her, sharing in her joy."

Zainab's eyes softened. "Sometimes, love doesn't need words; it's in those quiet

moments."

Farhan nodded. "And for a while, those stolen moments were enough."

And he continues at the entrance of the chai ki dukan, my heart pounding like a drum in my chest. The rain had slowed to a gentle drizzle, and the air was thick with the scent of wet earth and freshly brewed chai. I spotted Ayesha, her eyes twinkling with mischief, as she savored a jalebi with the same passion that had first captivated me.

Gathering my courage, I approached her table. "Excuse me," I began, my voice barely above a whisper. "Is this seat taken?"

Ayesha looked up, her lips curling into a playful smile. "Depends," she said, her eyes dancing with amusement. "Are you here for the chai or the jalebis?"

I chuckled nervously, feeling his cheeks flush. "Actually, I was hoping for some company," I admitted, my gaze dropping to the table.

"Well, you've come to the right place," Ayesha replied, her tone teasing. "But be warned, I don't share my jalebis."

My heart skipped a beat at her playful banter. "I wouldn't dream of it," I said, finally meeting her gaze. "But maybe you could tell me what makes them so special?"

Ayesha leaned back in her chair, her eyes never leaving his. "It's not just the taste," she said, her voice softening. "It's the way they make you feel. Like you're savoring a piece of happiness, one bite at a time."

I felt a warmth spread through him at her words. "I think I understand," I said, my voice steadying. "It's like finding joy in the little things."

Ayesha's smile widened, and she nodded. "Exactly. And sometimes, those little things can lead to something much bigger."

As the rain continued to fall outside, Ayesha and Me talked for hours, our conversation flowing as effortlessly as the monsoon rain. With each word, I felt my hesitation melt away, replaced by a growing connection that neither of them could deny.

As the evening wore on, the chai ki dukan became a cozy haven from the rain. Ayesha's and mine conversation flowed effortlessly, punctuated by laughter and the occasional teasing remark.

"So, Doctor Sahib," Ayesha said, her eyes sparkling with mischief. "Do you always spend your evenings at chai shops, or is this a special occasion?"

I smiled, feeling more at ease with each passing moment. "Well, I must admit, this place has become a bit of a favorite of mine recently," I said, his tone playful. "And I think I have you to thank for that."

Ayesha raised an eyebrow, her smile widening. "Oh really? And what makes you say that?"

I leaned in slightly, his voice dropping to a conspiratorial whisper. "Let's just say, there's something about the way you enjoy those jalebis that makes this place feel... magical."

Ayesha laughed, a sound that seemed to blend perfectly with the rhythm of the rain. "Magical, huh? That's quite a compliment coming from a doctor."

My heart raced as I watched her, captivated by her infectious energy. "It's true," he said, his voice sincere. "You have a way of making the ordinary seem extraordinary."

Ayesha's expression softened, and for a moment, the playful glint in her eyes was replaced by something deeper. "Thank you, Farhan," she said quietly. "That means a lot."

The two of us sat in comfortable silence for a while, the rain providing a soothing backdrop to ours thoughts. I felt a sense of contentment I hadn't experienced in a long time, simply being in Ayesha's presence.

As the evening drew to a close, l knew that this was just the beginning of something special. The connection I felt with Ayesha was undeniable, and I couldn't wait to see where their journey would take us next.

As the evening breeze carried the earthy scent of rain, I found myself drawn deeper into Ayesha's world. I admired her spirited laughter, which danced effortlessly with the fading sounds of the monsoon.

Curious to know more about her, I asked, "Ayesha, tumhe kya kya pasand hai? I

mean, what are the things that truly bring you joy?"

Ayesha's eyes sparkled as she leaned closer, her voice laced with enthusiasm. "Oh, bohot saari cheezein! Especially the street food of Lahore. Jitne bhi chezein Lahore ki galiyaan mein milte hain aur khayi ja sakti hain, un sabko main pasand hoon."

I couldn't help but smile at her exuberance. "Lahore ki galiyaan, huh? Sounds like a feast for the senses."

Ayesha nodded vigorously, her excitement infectious. "Yes! The spicy chaat, the succulent kebabs, the sweet and tangy golgappas... Each bite is like a celebration of life. There's a certain magic in the air of those bustling streets, and I love every bit of it."

As she spoke, I could envision the lively streets of Lahore, filled with the aroma of sizzling food and the vibrant energy of the city. Her passion for these simple joys made me see her in a whole new light.

"Sounds enchanting," Farhan said softly, his gaze never leaving hers. "Maybe one day, you can show me your favorite spots in Lahore?"

Ayesha's playful smile returned. "Maybe one day, I will. But for now, let's start

with the best jalebis right here."

I laughed, feeling a warmth that spread from my heart to his very soul. In that moment, under the dim light of the chai ki dukan, surrounded by the gentle patter of rain, I felt an unspoken promise in the air—a promise of many more shared moments, conversations, and perhaps, adventures to come.

The rain had slowed to a gentle drizzle outside, but inside the chai ki dukan, the atmosphere was charged with an electric warmth. I caught up in Ayesha's infectious excitement about Lahore's street food, decided to take a bold step.

I picked up a glistening jalebi from the plate and took a bite. The sweetness hit my senses immediately, but there was something more—something indescribable. It was as if the jalebi was laced with a magic I had never tasted before.

My eyes widened, and I looked at Ayesha in amazement. "Ayesha, yeh jalebi... it's unlike anything I've ever tasted. It's... different."

Her eyes twinkled with mischief as she leaned forward, a shy smile playing on her lips. "Oh, Doctor Sahib, you're in for a treat. This isn't just any jalebi. This is the secret recipe of this dukan. It's made with a pinch of love and a dash of magic."

I couldn't help but laugh at her playful exaggeration. "Magic, you say? Well, it certainly feels that way."

Ayesha's expression turned mock-serious. "Absolutely. Only the truly special can taste the magic. You see, these jalebis have a way of revealing what's hidden in one's heart."

My heart skipped a beat at her words, and he felt a strange mix of emotions— excitement, curiosity, and something deeper, something I couldn't quite name. "Well, if that's the case," I said softly, "I'm glad I tasted the magic."

Ayesha leaned back, satisfied with the impact of her words. "Who knows, Farhan? Maybe it's the start of something extraordinary."

The two of us shared a knowing look, the air around us crackling with unspoken possibilities. As I savored the last bite of the jalebi, I knew that this moment, this connection with Ayesha, was something rare and beautiful. It was a beginning, one that held the promise of countless shared moments, laughter, and perhaps, a touch of magic.

The rain had finally stopped, leaving the air fresh and cool. I Starts feeling a mix of excitement and nervousness, decided to seize the moment.

I mustered the courage to ask, "Do you come to this chai shop often?"

Ayesha's eyes sparkled with mischief as she replied, "Nahi, Doctor Sahib. Main aapke clinic bhi aa sakti hoon." Her playful tone made me laugh, easing the tension between us.

We shared a moment of laughter, the sound blending with the gentle rustle of leaves outside. I felt a warmth spread through him, a sense of connection that was growing stronger with each passing moment.

As she stood up to leave, Ayesha looked at Me with a knowing smile. "I should get going," she said softly. "But you know, there's this place in Lahore where they serve the most amazing chaat papdi on Sundays. And eating it under the moonlight... it doesn't taste like just chaat papdi, Doctor Sahib. Just like how your jalebi didn't taste like any ordinary jalebi."

I felt Like my heart skip a beat as her words lingered in the air, a sweet promise wrapped in playful mischief. Her enchanting presence and the magic of her words made me realize that this was just the beginning of something extraordinary. As I watched her walk away, I knew that Our story was just unfolding, filled with endless possibilities and the promise of many more

magical moments to come.

I stood there, the echo of Ayesha's words dancing in my mind. I couldn't help but smile at the playful charm she carried with her. She had a way of making even the simplest conversation feel like a grand adventure.

As I watched her walk away, she turned back one last time, her eyes gleaming with that same enchanting mischief. "Don't forget, Doctor Sahib," she called out, "this Sunday, under the moonlight. Trust me, the chaat papdi will taste like magic, just like your jalebi."

I felt a surge of anticipation. Her words held a promise of something more, something beyond the ordinary. I could already imagine the scene: the bustling streets of Lahore, the moon casting a gentle glow over the city, and the two of them sharing a moment under the stars.

As Ayesha disappeared into the night, I knew that our story was far from over. The rain had washed away the uncertainties, leaving behind a clear path filled with possibilities. And in the midst of it all, I found myself looking forward to every moment we would share, each one more magical than the last.

The next day, I was in my clinic, lost in thoughts of Ayesha and her enchanting tales of Lahore. I couldn't shake off her words about the magical chaat papdi

under the moonlight. As I attended some patients, and found myself wondering if such a place truly existed.

During a quiet moment, I decided to ask one of my regular patients, Mr. Kapoor, an elderly man with a wealth of local knowledge. "Mr. Kapoor," I began hesitantly, "do you know of a place where they serve chaat papdi on Sundays, and you can see the moon from there?"

Mr. Kapoor's eyes twinkled with amusement as he leaned back in his chair, stroking his beard thoughtfully. "Ah, Doctor Sahib, you're talking about Paratha Gali. It's a hidden gem," he said with a dramatic flair. "On Sunday nights, that place transforms into a culinary paradise. The chaat papdi there is legendary, but it's not just the taste—it's the experience."

My curiosity was piqued. "The experience?"

Mr. Kapoor nodded, his voice dropping to a conspiratorial whisper. "Yes, my boy. Imagine this the bustling streets filled with the aroma of freshly fried chaat, the laughter of families and friends, and above all, the moonlight casting a silver glow over everything. When you take that first bite of chaat papdi under the moon, it's like the flavors are enhanced by the magic of the night. You won't

just taste the chaat you'll feel it in your soul."

I smiled, My heart racing with anticipation. "That sounds incredible."

Mr. Kapoor chuckled. "It's more than incredible, Doctor Sahib. It's an experience that stays with you. You should take someone special there."

My thoughts immediately drifted to Ayesha, and I knew I had to see this place for myself. As Mr. Kapoor left, I felt a renewed sense of excitement. I couldn't wait to share this adventure with Ayesha, to experience the magic of Paratha Gali and the enchanting chaat papdi under the moonlight.

Sunday evening, I found myself wandering through the bustling Paratha Gali. I stood beneath each chaat papdi stall, craning my neck, searching for a

glimpse of the moon. But each time, disappointment followed.

Just as I was about to give up, I spotted a familiar figure sitting at a far-off stall. It was Ayesha, her presence like a beacon in the night. She seemed to glow under the dim lights, and I felt as though I was seeing her for the first time.

Drawn like a moth to a flame, l approached her, my heart pounding. When I

reached her, we greeted each other with a warm, "Salaam."

I, with a hint of playful frustration, said, "Yaha se chand toh nahi dikh raha."

Ayesha's eyes sparkled with mischief as she leaned closer. "Dikh toh raha hai, Doctor Sahib," she said, her voice teasingly soft. "Zara aap gaur se dekhiye."

l followed her gaze, and in that moment, I realized she wasn't talking about the moon in the sky. Her eyes, twinkling with that magical mischief, held all the light I needed. It was as if the world had fallen away, leaving just the two of us in our own universe.

My heart quickened as I finally understood Ayesha's playful hint. With a grin, I settled down beside her, our connection deepening with each passing moment. The world around us blurred as we delved into conversation, savoring the delicious chaat papdi and the unique magic of our encounter.

"You know, Ayesha," l began, "I never thought I'd find myself in a place like this, all because of a chance meeting in the rain."

Ayesha's eyes twinkled with that familiar mischief. "Life has a funny way of bringing people together, doesn't it? Just like the rain brought us to that chai ki dukan."

l nodded, my gaze fixed on her. "I'm glad it did. This feels... special."

Ayesha smiled, her expression softening. "It is, Farhan, these moments, the simple joys—they're what make life extraordinary."

As we continued to talk and laugh, the moon cast a silvery glow over Paratha Gali, making everything seem even more magical. For me, this was just the beginning of a beautiful journey with Ayesha, filled with endless possibilities and a love that transcended the ordinary.

As the days turned into weeks, Ayesha's and our' meetings became more frequent, our bond growing stronger with each encounter. We navigated the turbulence of the time, the whispers of partition ever-present, but our connection remained a source of solace and joy.

l often visited Ayesha's home, a quaint house where she lived with her mother. Her mother welcomed me with open arms, finding a kindred spirit in me. The

modest home became a sanctuary for our burgeoning love, a place where we could forget the world's chaos, even if just for a while.

One afternoon, the aroma of spices filled the air as Ayesha showed me how to cook. "You see, Doctor Sahib," she teased, "there's more to life than just treating patients. Cooking is an art, just like your medicine."

I a person, who had always been more comfortable with a stethoscope than a spatula, laughed nervously. "I'm not sure if I can manage this, Ayesha."

Ayesha's eyes sparkled with mischief as she handed him a ladle. "Nonsense! Today, you're not just a doctor. You're my sous-chef."

Under Ayesha's playful guidance, I learned how to cook Chicken Biryani and kheer. The process was filled with laughter and tender moments each step a testament to our growing bond. For me, it was a revelation the meticulous doctor was now discovering the joys of cooking, all thanks to Ayesha.

As we stood together in the kitchen, Ayesha's mother looked us with a smile. She saw the way Farhan's eyes softened when he looked at her daughter, and

the way Ayesha's laughter brightened the room. It was clear to her that this was no ordinary bond it was a love that could withstand even the harshest of times.

In those moments, amidst the whispers of partition and the uncertainty of the future, Ayesha and I found a sense of normalcy and hope. Our love story was not just about the sweetness of jalebis or the magic of chaat papdi it was about finding light in the darkest times and cherishing the simple joys that life had to offer.

Farhans gaze softened as he recounted his cherished memories to Zainab. "You know, Zainab, Ayesha was the first one who taught me how to cook. I was always the meticulous doctor, but in her presence, I became a novice chef. She showed me the magic in blending spices, the art of cooking that transcended mere recipes."

Zainab listened intently, her eyes wide with curiosity. Farhan continued, "And Ayesha loved to dance in the rain. I, being the cautious doctor, always tried to stop her. I would say, 'Ayesha, you'll catch a cold!' But she would just laugh, her eyes sparkling with mischief, and pull me into the rain with her."

A smile spread across Farhan's face as he remembered those moments. "She used to say, 'Doctor Sahib, these rains have a fragrance, a magic of their own.

You have to feel it, breathe it in.' And every time, I would find myself giving in, letting go of my reservations, and enjoying the rain with her."

Zainab could see the warmth in his eyes, the love that still lingered in his heart for Ayesha. Those memories, filled with laughter, rain, and the simple joy of being together, painted a vivid picture of a love that was both timeless and deeply cherished.

Farhan's eyes grew distant, as if he were transported back to those tumultuous days. He spoke softly, "Ayesha was always fearless, even as the whispers of partition grew louder. One evening, she held my hand tightly and led me through the winding streets of Lahore. There was an urgency in her steps, yet she exuded a calm strength."

"She turned to me and said, 'Farhan, it's just us now. My mother, you, and me. We're all we have.' Her voice was steady, but I could sense the weight of her words."

Zainab listened intently, feeling the emotion in Farhan's voice. He continued, "In that moment, my heart broke. The realization of the uncertainties we faced, the

dangers, and the sacrifices. But more than that, it was the fear of losing her—

the thought that our bond could be torn apart by forces beyond our control."

Farhan paused, the memories of those days hanging heavy in the air. "But even amidst the chaos, Ayesha never let go of my hand. Her fearless spirit and unwavering determination became my anchor. She showed me that love could endure, even in the darkest times."

"As Farhan continues telling his story to Zainab."

Our love story was a tapestry woven with vibrant threads of joy, laughter, and tenderness. Each moment we shared was a precious gem, glimmering even in the darkest times.

There were lazy afternoons spent in the garden, where Ayesha would read poetry aloud, her voice a melodic whisper that made my heart soar. we would sit under the shade of an old mango tree, sharing secrets and dreams, the world outside fading away.

We celebrated each other's birthdays with small, thoughtful gestures. On My birthday, Ayesha surprised him with a book of poetry, knowing how much I

loved words, she gifted me a handcrafted journal, its pages filled with her sketches and thoughts. "So you never forget the magic in the little things," she whispered, placing a gentle kiss on my forehead. I treasured that journal, each page a testament to her love and creativity.

We spent the evening reading verses to each other, Our laughter echoing in the quiet night.

On Ayesha's birthday, I surprised her with Bangles, adorned with tiny bells that jingled with her every step. Her eyes sparkled with delight as she fastened it around her ankle, and she danced around him, the bells creating a symphony of love and happiness. I decorated the garden with fairy lights and rose petals,

creating a magical ambiance. As she walked in, her eyes widened in delight. We danced under the stars, the world around Us disappearing into the background.

But our love wasn't without its trials. There were nights when the fears of partition loomed large, and we would hold each other close, whispering words of reassurance. I stroke Ayesha's hair, promising her that our love would endure, no matter the storms that raged around us.

One monsoon evening, we got caught in a sudden downpour. Ayesha, ever the spirited one, pulled me into the rain. "Feel it, Farhan," she laughed, twirling around me. "These rains have a fragrance, a magic that washes away all worries." And as we danced in the rain, soaked to the skin, I realized that my love for Ayesha was like the rain—wild, pure, and eternal.

Our bond deepened with each passing day, filled with countless shared moments. I cherished the way Ayesha would sneak into my clinic with homemade food, her smile lighting up my world. We steal moments between patients, sharing laughter and love amidst the chaos.

As the days grew shorter and the world around us changed, Ayesha's and mine love story continued to flourish. We found solace in each other, weaving our lives together with threads of hope and resilience.

One evening, as the golden hues of sunset bathed the city, I took her by the lake, where the moonlight danced upon the water's surface, each ripple shimmering like a thousand whispered secrets. The soft glow wrapped around us, casting an ethereal spell, and as the light touched the water, it seemed as if the stars themselves had fallen to the earth, sparkling at our feet. In that quiet moment, under the vast sky, the world faded, leaving only the two of us, bathed in the silver glow of the moon, surrounded by the beauty of nature's quiet romance.

We sat side by side, our hands intertwined, watching the water flow gently. "Ayesha," Farhan said softly, "no matter what happens, I want you to know that you are my anchor. You give me strength to face anything."

Ayesha smiled, her eyes filled with love. "And you, Farhan,' are my safe haven. With you, I feel like I can face any storm. Our moments together were a blend of joy and simplicity.

Our love story was also with full of challenges. There were days when the weight of the world seemed too much to bear. When I come home exhausted, the pressures of being a doctor in tumultuous times weighing heavily on me But Ayesha was always there, her presence a soothing balm to his weary soul. She would cook my favorite meals, her laughter filling our home with warmth and love.

And then there were the nights when we would sit together, the radio playing softly in the background, discussing our dreams and fears. The whispers of partition grew louder, and our future seemed uncertain. Yet, in each other's arms, we found a sense of security and hope.

One day, as we walked through the bustling streets of Lahore, as evening's golden light began to fade, she took my hand and led me quietly to a place I had never been before—a place sacred to her heart. In the soft, somber glow

of dusk, we arrived at her Abba's resting place. She stood beside the grave with a reverence that was almost tangible, her eyes shimmering as she looked upon it, as though she could still feel his presence beside her.

She turned to me, her voice low and steady, each word carrying a weight that seemed to fill the air around us. "My Abba," she said, her gaze softening, "was my strength, my guide. He was always there, telling me never to fear life, no matter how dark the path seemed. He taught me that there is always something to learn, something to hold on to, even in life's toughest moments."

I felt the strength in her words settle deep within me, as if her Abba's wisdom

had become part of her and, in that moment, part of me too.

And then, she reached into her little pouch, her hands delicate and graceful, as if handling a precious treasure. She pulled out a tiny bottle of perfume and pressed it gently into my hand. Her fingers lingered for a moment, warm against mine, before she let go.

Her voice softened, becoming almost a whisper. "When I'm not with you," she said, her eyes searching mine, "let this be my presence, my fragrance. Let it remind you that I am near, even when the world feels empty."

In that moment, I felt an inexplicable warmth, as if she were leaving a part of herself with me, entrusting me with a piece of her heart. The fragrance, delicate and familiar, filled the air around us, carrying her essence—her love, her courage, her unspoken promises.

As we stood there, surrounded by silence and memory, I knew that no matter where life would take us, her presence, her scent, her love would remain with me, woven into the very fabric of my being.

Our love was a beacon of light in a world filled with uncertainty. We cherished each moment, finding joy in the simplest of things. Whether it was dancing in the rain, cooking together, or sharing whispered conversations in the quiet of the night, our love remained strong and unbreakable.

Zainab sat quietly, her mind swirling with thoughts. The realization that she and Ayaan had shared the same gestures of love, even while separated by such vast distances, struck her deeply. It was as if their hearts were in sync, performing a delicate dance across the invisible threads that connected them.

As she thought about the bracelet she had given to Ayaan, the memory filled her with warmth and a touch of sorrow. She remembered how carefully she had chosen it, each bead and pattern holding a piece of her affection. The

knowledge that Ayaan cherished it as much as she cherished his gifts made her feel profoundly connected to him, despite the miles that lay between them.

In the mean time zainab often pondered how two souls in the same world could live such parallel lives yet be so far apart. The thought brought both comfort and agony, a stark reminder of the love they shared and the challenges they faced.

Zainab pulls herself out of her thoughts and begins to listen to Farhan's words

once again.

It's dusk, and the sky is ablaze with the colors of a setting sun. Ayesha and I meet at our secret spot near the old banyan tree, its ancient branches witnessing our love. The air is heavy with unspoken words. Ayesha, her eyes brimming with tears, finally musters the courage to speak her truth.

AYESHA: "Farhan, there's something you need to know. I've been hiding this

from you, but it's tearing me apart inside."

Farhan, sensing her distress, gently takes her hand.

FARHAN: "Ayesha, whatever it is, we can face it together."

Ayesha pulls her hand away, her tears now flowing freely.

AYESHA: She starts to cry, and through her tears, she whispers, "Do you even know my full name? My full name is Ayesha Kalal." Her voice trembles with sorrow, as if the weight of her words carries a lifetime of unspoken pain. The quiet despair in her eyes speaks of a longing for someone to see her, to know her entirely—not just the name, but the soul that bears it.

"I belong to the Kalal caste. I didn't tell you because I knew it would change everything.

I never told you this before because even I didn't know our bond would reach this far, so deep that it would consume every hidden corner of my heart. I was afraid... afraid that I might lose you if I shared this part of me. I couldn't bear the thought of you drifting away, leaving me alone with only memories that would forever haunt my soul. So, I kept silent, holding back, hoping it would be

enough to keep you close. But now... it hurts even more, knowing I had to hide

a piece of myself just to keep you near.

Your family... they'll never accept me. We can never truly be together."

The weight of her words hangs in the air, each syllable a dagger to my heart. I stands there, stunned, unable to find the words to bridge the chasm that has opened between Us.

FARHAN: "No... Ayesha, no. This can't be true. We love each other. That's what

matters."

Ayesha collapses into a sobbing heap, her cries echoing through the stillness.

AYESHA: "Love isn't enough, Farhan! Our world won't let us be together. It will

tear us apart, ruin our families. I can't bear to see you suffer because of me."

Farhan kneels beside her, his own tears now mixing with hers.

FARHAN: "But we can fight, Ayesha. We can find a way. I can't imagine a life without you."

Ayesha, still sobbing, shakes her head.

AYESHA: "Sometimes, love means letting go. You deserve a life free from this pain."

Ayesha stood before me, her heart pounding in my chest, the weight of her words almost suffocating. "Please, forgive me," she choked out, her voice trembling. "I never wanted to bring our relationship to this point. I didn't do this on purpose... I truly love you."

Tears cascaded down her cheeks, each drop a testament to the anguish she felt inside. She collapsed against my shoulder, her sobs racking her body as if the very essence of her sorrow was spilling out. My heart shattered at the sight of her pain. I instinctively wrapped my arms around her, holding her tightly as though i could shield her from the storm raging within.

"Don't cry, Ayesha," I murmured, my voice thick with emotion. "We will get

through this. We'll face every challenge together. You are everything to me."

As Farhan consoled her, his own heart ached. He felt the tears welling in his eyes, blurring his vision. He fought against them, determined to be her strength when she felt so weak. "No matter what happens, I'm here for you. Our love can conquer anything, even this despair."

Ayesha looked up at him, her eyes red and swollen, reflecting the deep sorrow

in her heart. "But what if I've already lost you?" she whispered, fear gripping her.

“No!” Farhan said fiercely, his resolve burning bright. “You haven’t lost me. We are meant to be, and I refuse to let anything tear us apart. I will fight for us, Ayesha, no matter how hard it gets.”

We stood there, wrapped in each other’s arms, both feeling the weight of their love and the pain of uncertainty.

She feels an overwhelming wave of sadness and guilt. She starts sobbing uncontrollably, the weight of her confession crashing down on her. Farhan, stunned and heartbroken himself, feels his own tears fall as he watches the love of his life in such anguish.

I tries to hold her, to provide some comfort, but Ayesha pulls away, shaking her head. She falls to the ground, her cries echoing in the silence of the night.

AYESHA: "How could I do this to us, Farhan? How could I hide something so important? I’ve ruined everything. I can never be Your family they will never accept me. I’ve shattered our dreams. Our love is doomed."

Farhan, kneeling beside her, his own heart breaking, reaches out to wipe away her tears.

FARHAN: "Ayesha, no... please don’t say that. Our love can overcome anything. I don’t care about castes or what society thinks. I just care about you. We can find a way. Together."

But Ayesha, sobbing harder, feels the weight of their impossible love pressing down on her chest. The pain is almost unbearable.

AYESHA: "It’s not that simple, Farhan. You don’t understand. The world won’t let us be together. Your families, our communities... they’ll never accept us. We’re fighting a losing battle."

I takes Ayesha’s hand in mine, with full of determination and love.

FARHAN: "Ayesha, I want you to listen to me carefully. I know our path isn't easy, but I promise you, I'll do everything in my power to make sure we're

together. I'll talk to my family, I'll make them understand. You belong with me, and I want you to come to my house as my bride."

Ayesha, her eyes wide with a mix of hope and fear, looks at Farhan.

AYESHA: "But Farhan, what if they don't accept us? What if they force you to choose between them and me?"

Farhan squeezes her hand tighter, his resolve unwavering.

FARHAN: "They will have to see how much you mean to me. I'll stand by you, no matter what. We'll fight this battle together. You're my future, Ayesha, and I won't let anyone take that away from us."

Tears of relief and love well up in Ayesha's eyes as she leans into Farhan's

embrace.

AYESHA: "I trust you, Farhan. I believe in our love. Just promise me you won't let

go, no matter how hard it gets."

FARHAN: "I promise, Ayesha. We'll face everything together. You and me, against the world.

She buries her face into his shoulder, feeling the weight of her emotions flow freely, as if pouring all her fears and unspoken love into him. His arms wrap around her even tighter, silently vowing to shield her from every shadow of loneliness. In that moment, they hold each other as though the world around them has faded away, leaving just the two of them—a fragile, heartbreaking beauty woven from love, longing, and the unspoken promises that lie between them.

The sun has set, casting long shadows across Farhan's family home. Inside, the atmosphere is tense as Farhan stands before his parents, his heart pounding with anxiety.

FARHAN: "Maa, Papa, I need to talk to you about something important."

His father, stern and unyielding, looks up from his newspaper.

FATHER: "What is it, Farhan?"

FARHAN: "It's about Ayesha. I love her, and I want to marry her."

His mother, already sensing the conflict, wrings her hands nervously.

MOTHER: "Farhan, you know how we feel about these things. Ayesha... she's

from a kalal caste."

FARHAN: "I know, Maa. But it doesn't matter to me. Ayesha is the one I want to spend my life with. She's kind, intelligent, and everything I've ever wanted in a partner."

His father's face hardens, his eyes cold.

FATHER: "Farhan, we have traditions and family honor to uphold. Marrying outside our caste is unacceptable.

Ayaan passionately explains that in Islam, the concept of caste is non-existent. Our Prophet Muhammad himself, advocating for a society rooted in equality and brotherhood. Islam emphasizes unity and the intrinsic worth of every individual, transcending the superficial barriers that divide people.

The teachings of Islam firmly state that no one is superior based on their lineage, wealth, or social status. Instead, piety and good deeds are what elevate

a person. This core belief is woven into the fabric of Muslim society, aiming to dismantle any remnants of caste-based discrimination. Ayaan's words echo the universal call of Islam for a just and equal society, reminding us of the profound wisdom in the Prophet's life and message.

Aayan's father, his voice firm and unyielding, looks him squarely in the eye, his tone carrying the weight of generations. "We will not allow a marriage outside of our caste," he declares, each word sharp as a blade. "Our family has lived by these traditions, and our place in society does not permit such defiance. If you insist on this path, then you must make a choice—a choice between us, your own blood, or that girl."

A tense silence fills the room, thick and suffocating, as his father's words cut deeper. "If you choose her, you will no longer belong to this family, and you need never set foot in this house again."

Aayan stands there, a storm of emotions raging within him. Torn between the love that has filled his soul and the roots that bind him to his family, he feels his heart splintering. His mind races through a lifetime of memories, every moment with his parents flashing before him, colliding with the promise of a future with her. The weight of his father's ultimatum hangs heavy, an impossible choice

between love and loyalty, leaving him with a decision that could shatter him forever.

Farhan feels the weight of his father's words like a crushing blow. He looks at his mother, seeking any sign of support.

MOTHER: "Your father is right, Farhan. This will bring shame to our family. Think about your future, about your responsibilities."

Farhan, tears welling up in his eyes, stands his ground.

FARHAN: "I love Ayesha, and I'm not willing to give up on her. I'll do whatever it

takes to make you understand."

His father slams the table, the sound echoing through the room.

FATHER: "Then you are no longer our son. Leave this house and don't come

back."

Farhan, heartbroken and devastated, turns to his mother one last time.

FARHAN: "Maa, please..."

But his mother, with tears in her eyes, looks away, unable to meet his gaze.

MOTHER: "I'm sorry, Farhan."

Farhan leaves the house, his heart shattered, knowing he's lost his family but determined to fight for his love. He walks to their secret spot, finding Ayesha waiting for him. As he reaches her, he collapses into her arms, sobbing uncontrollably.

FARHAN: "They disowned me, Ayesha. But I promised you... I'll never let go."

Ayesha, crying with him, holds him tightly.

AYESHA: "We'll face this together, Farhan. No matter what."

In the dim light of their secret spot, Farhan's tear-streaked face is full of hope and determination. Ayesha, her own eyes swollen with tears, gently cups his face, her heart breaking as she looks into his eyes.

AYESHA: "Farhan, I love you more than anything in this world. But I can't be the reason you lose your family. They mean everything to you, and I can't bear to see you suffer because of me."

Farhan, his voice choked with emotion, grasps her hands. FARHAN: "Ayesha, you are my life. I've already chosen you." Ayesha's tears fall freely now, her voice trembling with anguish.

AYESHA: "But Farhan, your family is your anchor, your identity. I can't take that away from you. The pain of losing them will haunt you forever. I can't bear to be the cause of that."

Farhan's grip tightens, desperation seeping into his voice.

FARHAN: "Ayesha, you are my family now. I'll endure anything to be with you. Please, don't push me away."

Ayesha, her sobs growing louder, shakes her head vigorously.

AYESHA: "No, Farhan. You don't understand. The bond with your family is sacred. It's irreplaceable. If you lose them for me, you'll always carry that sorrow. I can't live knowing I caused you that kind of pain."

Her body shakes with the force of her sobbing, her tears soaking into Farhan's shirt as she clings to him. The weight of her words pierces through Farhan's heart, and he too breaks down, the enormity of their situation crashing over him.

FARHAN: "But how can I live without you, Ayesha? How can I move on knowing we could have been together?"

Ayesha, choking on her tears, pulls back to look into his eyes, her heart shattering with every word.

AYESHA: "We have to be strong, Farhan. We have to believe that our love was meant to be, even if we can't be together. You'll find a way to heal. You'll find happiness again. And I'll carry your love in my heart forever."

Ayesha collapsing into Farhan's arms once more, both of them crying

uncontrollably.

The air is thick with sorrow, their sobs mingling with the silence of the night, a haunting symphony of a love lost to the cruel hands of fate.

The night is deep, the stars shimmering above as silent witnesses to the painful scene unfolding. Farhan and Ayesha, their faces streaked with tears, stand by the old banyan tree, their safe haven now a place of heartbreaking decisions.

AYESHA: "Farhan, you have to go back to your family. They need you, and you need them. I can't be the reason you lose them."

Farhan, his voice hoarse from crying, grabs Ayesha's hands, his eyes pleading.

FARHAN: "I can't, Ayesha. I can't leave you. Not like this. Our love is too strong to let go."

Ayesha, her heart breaking with every word, gently places her hand on his cheek.

AYESHA: "For me, Farhan... for the love we share. I'm asking you to go back. I

need you to be happy, even if it means being apart from me."

Farhan shakes his head, tears streaming down his face.

FARHAN: "No, Ayesha, please don't ask me to do this. I can't live without you."

Ayesha, her voice trembling, steps back, her resolve hardening through her tears.

AYESHA: "Then I give you my Kasam, Farhan. Promise me you'll go back to your family and fulfill their wishes. Promise me, for my sake, that you'll move on and find happiness."

Farhan, shattered by her words, falls to his knees, sobbing uncontrollably.

FARHAN: "Ayesha, no... don't do this. Please, I beg you."

Ayesha kneels down, her tears mingling with his, as she holds his face in her hands.

AYESHA: "Farhan, my love, this is the only way. Our love is eternal, but I can't watch you destroy yourself. Promise me, Farhan. For the love we have, promise me."

With a heart-wrenching cry, Farhan finally gives in, his voice breaking.

FARHAN: "I promise, Ayesha. I promise to go back and honor your wish."

They collapse into each other's arms, their sobs echoing through the night, knowing this might be their last embrace. The pain of their separation is palpable, their hearts breaking into a thousand pieces.

As Farhan walks away, his heart shattering with each step, Ayesha stands rooted to the spot, tears streaming down her face, watching the love of her life fade into the night.

In the background, ***"Tum Mere Paas Ho"*** begins to play, its haunting melody enveloping them both in a wave of sorrow:

Tum mere paas ho
Toh gham badi door ho ga
Kehata hai jiya mera re ,

Farhan pauses for a moment, looking back at Ayesha one last time, their eyes meeting across the distance.

As the final notes of the song linger in the air, Farhan turns and disappears into the darkness. Ayesha collapses to her knees, sobbing uncontrollably, the haunting melody a testament to their undying love and the cruel fate that has torn them apart.

Farhan sits with Zainab, his eyes filled with a mixture of sorrow and determination. The air is heavy with unspoken words, and Zainab can sense the turmoil within him.

FARHAN: "Zainab, there's something I need to tell you. When I agreed to marry you, it wasn't because I didn't care.

It's because Ayesha made me promise. She knew I couldn't lose my family, and she gave me her Kasam to ensure I wouldn't turn my back on them."

Zainab, taken aback, looks at him with a mixture of shock and compassion.

ZAINAB: "Farhan, I had no idea. Why didn't you tell me sooner?"

Farhan sighs, his heart aching with every word.

FARHAN: "Because I was torn between my love for Ayesha and my duty to my family. Even after our marriage, I kept trying to convince my parents to accept Ayesha. I couldn't bear the thought of living without her, knowing she was suffering because of me."

His voice breaks, and Zainab sees the depth of his pain. She reaches out, taking his hand in hers, her own heart heavy with empathy.

ZAINAB: "What did they say, Farhan?"

FARHAN: "Every time I brought it up, my parents refused to listen. They said they'd never accept a Kalals girl as their daughter-in-law. They threatened to disown me if I kept trying. It was like a knife to my heart every single time."

Tears well up in Farhan's eyes, and he continues, his voice trembling.

FARHAN: "I felt like I was being torn apart. On one side, my family, who raised me and gave me everything. On the other, Ayesha, the love of my life, who sacrificed her happiness for my sake. I didn't know what to do."

Zainab, with tears in her own eyes, squeezes his hand, her voice gentle yet firm.

Sitting across from Zainab, Farhan's eyes are shadowed with years of unspoken grief. The memories of Ayesha weigh heavily on his heart, and he takes a deep breath before speaking.

FARHAN: "Zainab, since the day Ayesha left my life, I've been drowning in

sorrow. I couldn't bear the emptiness, so I immersed myself in her family

business. This alcohol... it's the only thing that brings me any solace, any

reminder of her presence."

Zainab looks at him, her eyes filled with compassion and sadness. She sees the

pain etched into his features, the burden he's carried alone.

FARHAN: "Every bottle I touch, every drop I pour, it feels like a piece of Ayesha's spirit is still with me. This business, it's all I have left of her. When I drink, it's like I can almost hear her laughter, feel her warmth. It's the only way I know how to keep her memory alive."

His voice breaks, and tears start to fall. Zainab, moved by his raw emotion, reaches out to comfort him.

ZAINAB: "Farhan, you've been carrying this pain alone for so long. It's okay to grieve, to feel lost. But you don't have to do it alone anymore."

Farhan's hands shake as he holds the glass, his tears mingling with the alcohol.

FARHAN: "I know I should move on, but how can I? Every moment without her feels like a lifetime of torment. She was my everything, and now all I have are these fleeting reminders."

He looks at Zainab, his eyes pleading for understanding.

FARHAN: "The drinks... they're not just a business. They're my connection to her, my way of coping with this unbearable emptiness. Without them, I fear I'd lose the last piece of her I have left."

Zainab, her heart breaking for Farhan, nods gently.

ZAINAB: "We'll find a way to heal together, Farhan. We'll honor her memory

and find a way to move forward, side by side."

Farhan, filled with sorrow, looked at Zainab with eyes that seemed to hold a world of pain. "Zainab," he began, his voice breaking, "when I heard about Ayesha's death at the tea stall, my world ended right there."

His words hung heavy in the air, the raw emotion palpable. Zainab saw the anguish in his eyes, the devastation of a man who had lost his love. Farhan

continued, "She was everything to me. Hearing that she was gone... it felt like my heart was torn from my chest."

Tears welled up in Zainab's eyes as she listened. Farhan took a deep breath, his voice trembling. "You know, she was carrying the wedding dress she had dreamed of wearing herself. She was bringing it for you. Imagine the love she must have had, to part with something she cherished so deeply, just for your happiness."

The enormity of Ayesha's sacrifice hit Zainab like a tidal wave. The dress, now forever stained with Ayesha's blood, symbolized not only a lost love but also the selflessness and strength Ayesha had carried with her to her last breath.

Farhan's eyes filled with tears as he continued, "She sacrificed her dreams for you, Zainab. That wedding dress she carried—it was meant for her, something she dreamed of wearing on her own wedding day. But she was bringing it for you, knowing how much it meant for your happiness."

Zainab felt the weight of his words settle heavily on her heart. The realization of

Ayesha's sacrifice, her selflessness even in her final moments, was overwhelming. The red dress, now stained with Ayesha's blood, symbolized a love and friendship that transcended even death. It was a poignant reminder of the intertwined fates and the deep connections between all of them.

In the silence that followed, the shared grief between Farhan and Zainab

became a bridge, linking their sorrows and memories of Ayesha. The complexity of their emotions, the shared loss, and the tragic beauty of Ayesha's selfless act painted a heart-wrenching picture of love and sacrifice.

Zainab, her eyes shimmering with unshed tears and heart swelling with the weight of Ayesha's sacrifice and Farhan's pain, took a deep breath. She reached out, gently clasping his hands in hers, her touch tender and full of quiet

strength. Her voice was soft but carried the weight of her conviction.

"Farhan," she began, her voice trembling slightly, "promise me. Promise me that from today onwards, you will never touch a drop of alcohol again. Not just for yourself, but for Ayesha and the love she had for both of us."

Farhan's facade of strength crumbled at her words. He had always been the stoic one, but in this moment, the dam of his emotions broke. Tears welled up in his eyes, spilling over and running down his cheeks. He fell to his knees, his shoulders shaking with the intensity of his sobs.

"I promise," he choked out, his voice raw with emotion. "I promise, Zainab. For

Ayesha, and for you."

Zainab knelt beside him, wrapping her arms around him in a comforting embrace. They held each other tightly, their tears mingling as they shared their grief and pain. The weight of their shared loss and the depth of their love for Ayesha bound them together in that moment.

As they clung to each other, Zainab whispered, "We will honor her memory, Farhan. We will carry her love with us, always."

Farhan nodded, unable to speak through his tears. In that moment, they found solace in each other's arms, their hearts united by the love and sacrifice of a dear friend. The promise they made to each other was a testament to the strength of their bond and their commitment to cherish Ayesha's memory forever.

ÞÞÞ

SIX

WINDS OF CHANGE

As time passes , Zainab began to lose hope in her search for Ayaan. Despite looking everywhere, there was no sign of him. The man who used to drown himself in alcohol, Farhan, had changed completely. He took care of Zainab, attending to her every need. Gradually, Zainab began to rely on him for solace, as he helped ease her pain.

At this point in her life, Zainab felt a void in her heart. She knew she would never get the answers to her questions. Why hadn't Ayaan returned? This question haunted her constantly. But now, Farhan's love and support brought a new light into her life. Slowly, Zainab began to accept this reality, understanding the new chapter that had opened for her.

Zainab's heart now carried a new pain—the pain of an incomplete love story. She couldn't understand why Ayaan never came back. This truth broke her heart, but Farhan's companionship gave her the strength to keep going.

Now, Zainab and Farhan had become each other's pillars of support. Their story had taken a new direction.

As the days turned into weeks, Farhan found himself increasingly drawn to Zainab. His admiration for her quiet strength and resilience grew with each passing moment. Every time he saw her, his heart would flutter with an unfamiliar, yet exhilarating sensation. He had initially started caring for her out of a sense of duty and shared grief, but now, those feelings were evolving into something deeper.

Farhan's mind often wandered, imagining a future with Zainab. He pictured her smile, the way her eyes would light up when she spoke of something she was passionate about. He found himself yearning to be the reason behind that smile, to be the one who brought joy and comfort into her life.

One evening, as they sat together in the dim glow of the lantern, Farhan couldn't help but steal glances at Zainab. She was engrossed in her thoughts, her delicate features bathed in the soft light. In that moment, Farhan realized just how much she meant to him. The mere thought of her brought warmth to his heart, and he felt a deep desire to protect her, to cherish her.

Zainab, sensing his gaze, looked up and their eyes met. For a fleeting moment, time seemed to stand still. Farhan's breath caught in his throat, and he saw a flicker of emotion in her eyes. It was a silent acknowledgment of the bond that had formed between them, a bond that was growing stronger with each passing day.

He often found himself daydreaming about her, imagining the two of them walking hand in hand through the market, sharing laughter and secrets. He dreamed of waking up to her smile, of building a life together filled with love and understanding. The more he thought about it, the more his heart ached with the longing to make those dreams a reality.

As Farhan's feelings deepened, he became even more attentive to Zainab's needs. He would bring her flowers, small tokens of his affection, hoping to bring a smile to her face. He listened to her, offering comfort and support, and in those moments, he felt a connection that went beyond words.

Farhan's feelings for Zainab grew stronger, a tender, yet powerful force that filled his heart. It was a love born out of shared sorrow, but now it was blossoming into something beautiful and pure. He was determined to stand by her side, to be her strength, just as she had unknowingly become his.

Farhan sat quietly, lost in thought. His mind wandered back to the night of the engagement when he first saw Zainab through the delicate veil of her ghoonghat. The soft glow of the lantern had cast a gentle light on her face, and in that moment, she looked ethereal, like a vision from his dreams. He remembered feeling a rush of emotions, the dreams and hopes of a lifetime flooding his heart.

He had imagined their life together, dreaming of moments filled with love and joy. But back then, the reality had been different. Zainab had needed a friend, a pillar of support to lean on through her grief. Farhan had stepped into that role, setting aside his own dreams for the sake of her well-being.

But now, as the days turned into weeks and their bond grew stronger, Farhan couldn't help but feel that perhaps those dreams were not as unattainable as he once thought. He imagined Zainab in her bridal attire, walking towards him with the same grace and beauty that had captivated him that night. The softness in her eyes, the gentle smile playing on her lips—it all felt so real.

In his daydreams, he saw them together, with Farhan gently running his fingers through Zainab's hair, the world around them fading away. He pictured them laughing together, their hands intertwined as they walked through the bustling streets, sharing secrets and dreams. Farhan's heart swelled with love and hope, the thought of building a life with Zainab filling him with warmth.

He recalled the dreams he had once had—dreams of waking up to her smile, of creating a home filled with love and laughter. Farhan could now see those dreams taking shape, becoming a beautiful reality. The more he thought about it, the more he believed that their love had the power to heal, to transform their lives and make their dreams come true.

As he watched Zainab from across the room, his heart ached with longing. She was no longer just a friend in need she became the woman of his affection , the one he wanted to spend the rest of his life with. Farhan's eyes softened as he imagined their future together—a future where their love would grow stronger with each passing day.

With every passing moment, Farhan's resolve grew firmer. He knew that he would do everything in his power to make those dreams a reality, to cherish and protect Zainab, and to build a life filled with love and happiness together.

Farhan found himself consumed by a whirlwind of emotions. The feelings he harbored for Zainab had grown into something profound and deep, but with those emotions came a torrent of self-doubt. He questioned whether what he felt for her was right, or if he was simply projecting his own desires onto her.

Sitting alone in his room, Farhan couldn't shake off the nagging thoughts. He wondered if by expressing his feelings, he might break the delicate trust Zainab had placed in him. The thought of losing her, not just as a potential partner but as a dear friend, gnawed at his heart.

His mind was a tumultuous sea of worries. "What if Zainab doesn't feel the same way?" he pondered. "What if she sees me only as a friend, someone she

depends on for support?" The fear of rejection loomed large, casting a shadow over the affection he felt. He remembered the moments they'd shared, the way her eyes would light up in his presence, but even those memories were tainted by doubt.

Farhan sighed deeply, the weight of his uncertainty pressing down on him. He didn't want to jeopardize the bond they had built, the fragile connection that had been their solace through so much pain. "Is it selfish of me to want more?" he questioned himself, his heart aching with the possibility.

The fear of breaking Zainab's trust was almost unbearable. She had confided in him, leaned on him through her darkest moments, and the thought of causing her more pain was unfathomable. "What if my feelings push her away?" Farhan thought, his chest tightening at the idea of losing her completely.

His mind wandered to the dreams he'd dared to entertain—the tender moments of holding Zainab's hand, the shared laughter, the future they could build together. But now, those dreams felt precarious, like a fragile glass that could shatter with a single misstep.

Farhan's heart was torn between his longing and his fear. He yearned to tell Zainab how he felt, to open his heart to her, but the risk seemed too great. He feared that by acting on his feelings, he might lose the one person who had come to mean everything to him.

In that moment of vulnerability, Farhan made a silent vow. He would cherish the bond they had, protect it with all his heart, and put Zainab's happiness above

his own. Even if it meant keeping his feelings hidden, he would do whatever it took to ensure she never felt betrayed or burdened by his emotions.

Farhan knew that the path ahead was uncertain, but he was willing to navigate it with patience and care. His love for Zainab was steadfast, and he resolved to be her strength, her unwavering support, no matter what.

In the quiet solitude of his room, Farhan found himself lost in a sea of emotions. His fingers trembled as he opened a small wooden box, revealing the ring he had once given to Zainab on their wedding night. The delicate piece of jewelry shimmered softly in the dim light, a symbol of promises made and dreams unfulfilled.

As he held the ring, memories of that night flooded back. He remembered the way Zainab had looked, her face partially hidden behind the ghoonghat, her eyes shining with a mix of hope and apprehension. Farhan had slipped the ring onto her finger, his heart swelling with the belief that they were about to embark on a beautiful journey together.

But now, as he gazed at the ring, those dreams felt fragile and distant, like wisps of smoke that could disappear at any moment. Farhan's heart ached with a mixture of love and sorrow, the weight of his feelings pressing heavily on his chest. He couldn't help but imagine what it would be like to place the ring on Zainab's finger once more, to see her accept it with a smile that reached her eyes.

In his mind, he envisioned Zainab standing before him, her eyes filled with warmth and affection. He could almost feel the softness of her hand as he gently slipped the ring onto her finger, their bond reaffirmed in that simple, yet

profound gesture. Farhan's heart fluttered with the hope that this time, Zainab would accept him not out of obligation, but out of genuine love.

Each day spent by Zainab's side had deepened his feelings for her. He had watched her navigate through her grief, her strength and resilience shining through. His admiration for her had grown into something more, a love that was both tender and fierce. Farhan found solace in the thought that perhaps, with time, Zainab's heart might come to mirror his own.

But along with hope came a gnawing fear. Farhan worried that his feelings might not be reciprocated, that he could lose the trust and friendship they had built. The thought of causing Zainab any more pain was unfathomable. He didn't want his love to become a burden, to push her away when all he wanted was to be closer to her.

As he held the ring, Farhan's mind raced with conflicting emotions. He knew that their bond had grown stronger with each passing day, but the uncertainty of Zainab's feelings left him feeling vulnerable and fragile. The fear of rejection loomed large, casting a shadow over his dreams.

Yet, despite the doubts and fears, Farhan couldn't help but hold onto the hope that their love could flourish. He believed in the strength of their connection,

the unwavering support they had given each other. Farhan resolved to cherish the moments they shared, to nurture the love that had blossomed in his heart.

With a deep breath, Farhan placed the ring back in the box, his mind filled with visions of a future where Zainab stood by his side, their love a beacon of hope and resilience. He knew that the journey ahead would be uncertain, but he was determined to face it with courage and unwavering devotion.

With just a month left until February 4th, Farhan was filled with a mix of excitement and nervous anticipation. This date marked their second wedding anniversary, a stark contrast to their first. On their first anniversary, they barely knew each other, having been married more out of necessity than love. There was nothing special about that day—just a quiet acknowledgment of their bond and a shared meal, with Farhan seeing Zainab more as a friend who needed his help than anything else.

But now, a year later, everything had changed. Farhan's feelings for Zainab had deepened into a profound love, and he was determined to make this anniversary one to remember. He wanted to show Zainab just how much she meant to him and how she had become the light in his life.

As the days passed, Farhan meticulously planned how he would make their second anniversary special. He thought about the words he would use to tell her how she had transformed his life, bringing hope and love into it. He imagined a beautiful evening filled with heartfelt moments, hoping to convey the depth of his feelings.

He also prepared himself for the possibility that Zainab might not feel the same way. He decided that if she didn't share his feelings, he would reassure her that their friendship would remain intact. "If you don't feel the same, we will always be best friends, and I need nothing more than your happiness," he rehearsed in his mind.

Farhan remembered the first night they spent together as husband and wife, how they were both filled with uncertainty and the weight of their circumstances. But now, he felt a deep connection to Zainab, not because of the circumstances that brought them together, but because of the love he felt for her as a person. He was ready to confess this love, to let her know how much she had come to mean to him.

He often found himself daydreaming about placing the ring back on her finger, hoping she would accept it with a genuine smile this time. Each passing day made his feelings for Zainab grow stronger, and he was filled with hope that their love could flourish.

As the days led up to their anniversary, Farhan noticed that every little thing Zainab did for him seemed like a scene from a romantic Bollywood movie. Whenever she brought him tea or laughed at one of his jokes, he couldn't help but feel like a melody was playing softly in the background. He often found himself daydreaming, imagining Zainab and himself as the protagonists of a beautiful love story.

One evening, as Zainab brought him a cup of tea, Farhan's mind drifted to the lyrics of a romantic song. He saw them dancing together, lost in each other's eyes, their hearts beating as one. The song played on, filling his mind with images of a future where they were together, happy and in love.

The song that seemed to play in the background of his mind was

" ***Main dil ka raaz kehta hoon, ki jab jab saansein leta hoon, Teri baatein karta hoon*** "...

The lyrics resonated deeply with his feelings, as if the words were written just for him .

Farhan's heart ached with the desire to make those dreams come true. He watched Zainab with a tender smile, his feelings for her growing stronger with each passing day. The thought of telling her everything on their anniversary filled him with a mix of excitement and nervousness, but he knew that he had to follow his heart.

As February 4th approached, Farhan prepared himself for the moment when he would finally open up to Zainab. He hoped that she would understand the

depth of his feelings, and that their love story would continue to unfold like the beautiful song that played in his mind.

February 4th finally arrived, a day that held so much significance for Farhan. The air seemed to hum with a special energy, and his heart beat faster with both excitement and a hint of nervousness. He had planned a beautiful evening for Zainab, determined to make this anniversary one that they would remember forever.

Farhan decorated their small home with lights and flowers, creating an atmosphere filled with warmth and love. He carefully prepared a meal with all of Zainab's favorite dishes, wanting every detail to reflect his love and appreciation for her. As he set the table, his mind kept drifting back to the song that had been playing in his thoughts for weeks:

Main dil ka raaz kehta hoon,

ki jab jab saansein leta hoon, Teri baatein karta hoon,

When Zainab walked into the room, she was taken aback by the transformation. The soft glow of the lights, the sweet fragrance of the flowers, and the

beautifully set table—it all took her breath away.

And in Farhans background melody of a song play's

" Main Agar Saamne Aa Bhi Jaaya Karoon

Laazmi Hai Ki Tum Mujhse Parda Karo "

She looked at Farhan, her eyes filled with a mix of surprise and emotion.

Farhan, unable to contain his feelings any longer, took a deep breath and walked over to her. "Zainab," he began, his voice filled with tenderness, "you have been my strength, my hope, and my light. Over the past year, my feelings for you have grown deeper than I ever imagined. Not because of the circumstances, but because of the amazing person you are."

He reached into his pocket and pulled out the ring, the same one he had given her on their wedding night. "This ring was a promise I made to you when we barely knew each other. Today, I want to renew that promise, not out of obligation, but out of love."

As he gently slipped the ring onto her finger, Farhan's heart raced with anticipation. He looked into her eyes, hoping to see a reflection of his own feelings. "No matter what, Zainab, I want you to know that you mean the world to me. If you don't feel the same, we can remain the best of friends. But I had to tell you how I truly feel."

Zainab's eyes filled with tears, overwhelmed by the depth of Farhan's words and the sincerity in his eyes. She felt a surge of emotions, memories of their journey together flooding her mind. The love and care Farhan had shown her, the way he had stood by her side through everything—it all came crashing down in a wave of realization.

Without a word, she wrapped her arms around him, holding him close. Farhan felt her tears on his shoulder and knew that whatever her response, they had crossed a significant threshold in their relationship.

The sound of the alarm clock jolts Farhan awake. He blinks a few times, disoriented, and glances over at the clock. **It's 8:00 AM of February 3rd.** Realization dawns on him—everything he had just experienced was a dream. The heartfelt confession, the romantic evening, the song playing in the background—it was all a vivid dream. Farhan lets out a soft laugh, his heart still racing from the intensity of it all.

As he sits up in bed, a smile spreads across his face. The dream felt so real, and it fills him with a sense of purpose and excitement. "Maybe this is a sign," he thinks to himself, "a sign to make tomorrow as special as I imagined in my dream."

Farhan decides then and there that he will plan the perfect surprise for Zainab on their second wedding anniversary. It will be a day filled with love and happiness, just as he had envisioned. He gets out of bed, feeling a renewed sense of energy and determination. It's as if his dream has given him a glimpse of what could be, and he is eager to make it a reality.

He spends the day preparing, putting his heart and soul into every detail. He decorates their small home with twinkling lights and fragrant flowers, creating

an ambiance of warmth and romance. He carefully plans the menu, choosing all of Zainab's favorite dishes and even attempting some new recipes to surprise her.

Farhan's mind keeps drifting back to the lyrics of the song from his dream, "Main Dil Ka Raaz Kehta Hoon." The words echo in his thoughts, filling him with a sense of hope and anticipation. He imagines the look on Zainab's face when

she walks into the room, the joy and surprise in her eyes. The thought makes his

heart flutter, and he can't help but hum the tune as he works.

Throughout the day, Farhan finds himself thinking about the dream, how vivid and real it had felt. He takes it as a positive sign from God, a hint that his plans for their anniversary will be successful. The dream has shown him what he truly wants, and he is determined to make it happen.

As he cooks, Farhan's mind is filled with images of Zainab—her smile, her laughter, the way she lights up the room. He imagines dancing with her, lost in the music, their hearts beating in sync. The thought of holding her close, of whispering his feelings to her, fills him with a sense of excitement and nervousness.

Every little thing Zainab does that day seems to reinforce his determination. Whenever she brings him tea or shares a laugh, Farhan feels the connection between them growing stronger. He can't wait to tell her how he feels, to let her know just how much she means to him.

As the day draws to a close, Farhan takes a moment to admire his handiwork. The lights, the flowers, the food—all of it is a labor of love, a testament to his feelings for Zainab. He knows that tomorrow will be a special day, one that they will both remember for years to come.

With a hopeful heart and a determined spirit, Farhan prepares himself for the most important day of his life. He knows that whatever happens, he will cherish the moment and the love they share. Tomorrow will be the beginning of a new chapter, filled with love, hope, and happiness.

The day of February 4th finally arrives. Farhan has spent hours decorating their small home, transforming it into a romantic haven filled with twinkling lights and fragrant flowers. The table is set with all of Zainab's favorite dishes, each detail meticulously planned to perfection. His heart races with anticipation, his mind filled with dreams of the perfect evening.

With everything ready, Farhan takes a deep breath and heads to find Zainab. His emotions swirl within him—hope, excitement, and a hint of nervousness. He approaches her room, a soft smile playing on his lips, ready to invite her to the beautifully decorated living room.

As he reaches Zainab's room, he sees her sitting by the window, her gaze distant and filled with melancholy. She seems lost in another world, her sadness palpable. Farhan feels a pang of worry, thinking that perhaps Zainab is still haunted by the past. But he pushes those thoughts aside, determined to bring joy into her life. "After today, she will never feel alone again," he thinks to himself. "I will give her all the happiness she deserves."

Little does Farhan know, Zainab's mind is also consumed with thoughts of him. She has been reflecting on their journey together, thinking about how Farhan has been her pillar of strength and support. Her heart swells with admiration

and gratitude for him. She realizes that she has come to care deeply for Farhan, and maybe, just maybe, it's time to start a new chapter in her life with him.

Tears well up in Zainab's eyes as she thinks about how much Farhan means to her. She silently praises him for his kindness, his unwavering support, and the love he has shown her. She feels a rush of emotions, a mix of sorrow and hope, as the realization dawns on her that she wants to build a future with him.

Farhan, still standing by the door, calls her name softly. "Zainab," he says, his voice filled with warmth and affection. She turns to look at him, her eyes glistening with tears. Farhan feels his heart skip a beat, the intensity of the moment overwhelming him.

After seeing this seen, he realized that Zainab needed a bit of strength in her life. While watching her quietly, he thought about one of his patients—a remarkable man who had faced many struggles with a strength that Farhan deeply admired. This man, though scarred, had never given up. Farhan felt that if Zainab met him, maybe some of that courage could spark in Zainab too, helping her find her own inner strength again.

He decided that Zainab should meet him before they start a new chapter in their lives, hoping it might inspire her. Farhan felt a quiet determination, thinking that this meeting might bring her a sense of motivation and help fix everything.

SEVEN

THE DESTINY

Come with me, Farhan says gently, extending his hand towards her. Zainab hesitates for a moment before placing her hand in his. He leads her to the living room, the soft glow of the lights casting a magical ambiance around them. Zainab is taken aback by the transformation, her heart swelling with emotion.

He says softly, his voice filled with warmth and determination. "I want you to meet someone." As they walk through the quiet hallways, Farhan explains, "There's a patient of mine who has been bedridden for the past two years. A few days back, his condition started to improve, and we're hopeful he will fully recover soon. Despite everything, he hasn't given up on life. He's a fighter, knowing he must keep moving forward, no matter what."

Farhan's thoughts drift to the patient, a man whose resilience has always inspired him. "You know, Zainab, this patient of mine doesn't speak much. But in the last two years, he's said a few things that have stayed with me. He once told me, 'In another world, I'll be waiting.' Another time, he mentioned, 'We will dance in the first rain as we decided.'"

As Farhan speaks, Zainab listens intently, her heart touched by the story. Little does Farhan know, these very words send shockwaves through her. Her heartbeat quickens, her mind spinning, for these were the exact words Ayaan had written to her in his last letter. A mix of emotions—shock, sadness, and a glimmer of hope—rushes over her, leaving her breathless.

While they walk towards the hospital, Farhan silently reflects on his own feelings. He thinks about how, after introducing Zainab to his inspirational patient, he will finally share his heart with her and start a new life together. The anticipation builds within him, a blend of excitement and nervousness about the step he's about to take.

Reaching the patient's room, Farhan gently pushes open the door. The room is filled with a gentle light, and the patient lies there with a peaceful aura around him. Farhan softly calls out, and the man opens his eyes, a faint smile appearing.

"This is Zainab," Farhan says, his voice gentle but filled with emotion. "She means a lot to me, and I wanted her to meet someone who inspires me every day."

As the patient turns his face towards Zainab and Farhan, Zainab's breath catches in her throat. Her eyes widen as she recognizes the familiar features of the man she once loved dearly. Her heart races, pounding against her ribcage as memories flood her mind. Tears begin to well up in her eyes, and her vision blurs. She takes a shaky step forward, her voice barely a whisper.

In disbelief, she whispers, "Ayaan...?" Her voice cracks, the single word laced with a mixture of joy and pain. Her knees feel weak, and she ways, her hand clutched tightly around Farhan's as if anchoring herself from the whirlpool of emotions flooding her.

Farhan looks at her, startled, unable to fully comprehend what's unfolding. His brows knit in confusion, as he glances between Zainab and Ayaan, realization dawning slowly.

Zainab stumbles forward, releasing Farhan's hand, and falls to her knees beside Ayaan's bed, her trembling hands reaching out to touch his face. Tears spill down her cheeks, each one carrying the weight of years of longing, of words left unspoken, of love lost and now found.

With her voice choked with sobs, she says, "You... you came back. I thought... I

thought I'd lost you forever."

Ayaan's smile grows, his eyes filled with a mix of sorrow and joy. "Zainab," he whispers, his voice weak but filled with love, "I told you... in another world, I'll be waiting."

Ayaan's hand, weak yet resolute, lifts to rest upon hers, his fingers tracing her skin with a familiarity that defies the years apart. His gaze, soft yet intense, speaks volumes without a single word. They stare into each other's eyes, memories flooding back—shared dreams, promises made, and moments stolen beneath a rain-filled sky.

Zainab sobs, her heart aching with the pain of lost time and the joy of reunion. Farhan stands silently beside them, his own heart heavy with emotion, witnessing the profound connection between them. He realizes in that moment the depth of their bond and the unspoken love that has endured despite the years and distance.

Farhan steps back, his heart heavy, a sense of bittersweet understanding settling over him. In that moment, he knows that his own hopes, his dreams of a life

with Zainab, have been intertwined with a love that was never his to claim.

Farhan realize as if his entire world crumbles around him. Every dream he had woven with her, each one crafted with the tender threads of hope and

devotion, begins to unravel right before his eyes. His heart, once so full of silent promises, suddenly feels hollow, echoing with the ache of shattered love.

A lone tear escapes, trailing down his cheek, unbidden and uncontrollable. For the first time, he feels truly lost, adrift in a storm of emotions he never prepared for. The realization sinks deep, the love he dreamed of sharing with Zainab had already found its way into another's arms.

As he stands there, overwhelmed by the weight of his shattered dreams, his mind replays every precious moment he shared with Zainab. The gentle touch

of her hand, the warmth of her smile, the laughter they shared—it all feels like a cruel illusion now, slipping through his fingers like grains of sand.

Zainab, oblivious to the silent storm raging within Farhan, is bathed in the glow of her own happiness. She has found her love, her mohabbat, while his had barely taken its first breath before it was silenced. Farhan's heart breaks in that instant, knowing that the story he'd written in the language of his soul would remain forever incomplete, a half-spoken vow that would never be answered.

He watches as Zainab rushes to Ayaan's side, tears of joy streaming down her face. Her happiness is a stark contrast to the agony that grips Farhan's heart. The love he had nurtured so carefully, the dreams he had dared to dream, are now rendered meaningless in the face of this devastating truth.

In the depths of his despair, Farhan struggles to find a way to cope with the overwhelming pain. He feels like a stranger in his own life, the future he had envisioned slipping away into the shadows. The ache in his chest is a constant reminder of the love he had hoped to share with Zainab, now forever out of reach.

He tries to muster the strength to smile, to show his support for Zainab, but the effort feels impossible. His soul is shattered, the fragments of his heart scattered like broken glass. In the quiet recesses of his mind, he whispers a silent farewell to the dreams he had cherished, knowing that he must find a way to move forward, even if it means letting go of the love he held so dearly.

The stark contrast between Zainab's radiant joy and Farhan's silent suffering paints a heartbreaking picture of love unfulfilled and dreams left undone. Farhan's heart is left aching, a hollow void where hope once resided, knowing that his love story will remain a beautiful but tragic chapter in the book of his life.

As he thinks about the beautifully decorated home, filled with lights and flowers for Zainab, it now feels like a bitter mockery. He had envisioned this night as the beginning of their new life, but it was never meant to be. The image of the room, once full of warmth and promise, is now a painful reminder of his unfulfilled dreams.

Farhan's thoughts drift to the ring he had carefully kept in his pocket, meant to symbolize his unwavering love and commitment. With trembling hands, he reaches into his pocket and pulls out the ring. The sight of it brings a fresh wave of sorrow. He had imagined slipping it onto Zainab's finger, seeing her smile with genuine happiness. But now, that vision is nothing more than a cruel illusion.

As he stares at the ring, tears blur his vision. The pain of his unfulfilled dreams, the ache of a love that was never realized, crushes him. He clutches the ring tightly, his sobs wracking his body. The silent promises he had made to himself, the hopes he had nurtured, now lie in ruins. The ring, a symbol of his love, now feels like a weight pulling him down into the depths of his sorrow.

Farhan, fighting back the tidal wave of emotions crashing over him, takes a deep breath. His voice quivers with a mixture of tenderness and resolve as he turns to Zainab. "Zainab, let Ayaan rest now. He's yours, and I will protect what is yours until I can reunite you both," he says, his heart shattering with each word.

Zainab, overwhelmed by the depth of his sacrifice and the unspoken love in his eyes, stands up and embraces Farhan. The intensity of their embrace speaks volumes—an unspoken understanding, a mutual acknowledgment of the sacrifices they've both made. Tears stream down their faces, mingling together as they sob uncontrollably, finding solace in each other's arms.

Farhan holds her tightly, feeling the weight of his unfulfilled dreams and the love he had so desperately hoped to share. His heart aches with a pain so profound, yet he finds strength in Zainab's embrace. In that moment, he vows to protect her and Ayaan, no matter the cost.

Zainab's tears flow freely, her heart breaking for the man who has stood by her side, offering her unwavering support and love. She clings to Farhan, feeling the warmth of his embrace and the depth of his devotion. Her gratitude and sorrow blend together, creating a powerful bond between them.

In the silence of their shared grief, they find a fragile comfort. They are bound by their love for Ayaan, and by the promises they have made to each other. Farhan's heart swells with a bittersweet mixture of love and loss, knowing that his dreams will remain unfulfilled, but finding solace in the knowledge that he has given Zainab the happiness she deserves.

The room seems to hold its breath, witnessing the raw emotions and the silent vows exchanged between Farhan and Zainab. Their tears continue to fall, each drop a testament to the depth of their feelings and the sacrifices they have made. In that moment, they find a fragile strength in each other, a promise to face the future together, no matter how uncertain it may be.

Farhan, with his heart heavy and emotions swirling, gently leads Zainab back home. As they step inside, he guides her towards the room he had so lovingly decorated. The room is a beautiful testament to his feelings, filled with twinkling lights and fragrant flowers, an ambiance of love and devotion.

As Zainab enters the room, her eyes fall upon the table. The sight of the dishes, now cold and untouched, hits her like a wave. Each dish, carefully prepared with love, now seems like a silent witness to the dreams Farhan had nurtured. The room, adorned with decorations, speaks volumes of his efforts to make this

night special.

Zainab's tears begin to flow uncontrollably as the weight of the situation crashes down upon her. She can feel the depth of Farhan's love and the pain he must

be feeling. The beauty of the decorations and the cold dishes stand in stark contrast to the storm of emotions raging within them.

Farhan, his voice choked with sorrow, manages to say, "Happy second anniversary, Zainab, and also the last between us." The words hang in the air, filled with a mix of love and heartbreak. His tears flow freely, his heart aching with the realization that this night, meant to be a celebration of their union, has turned into a farewell.

Unable to contain her own emotions, Zainab rushes to Farhan and wraps her arms around him. They hold each other tightly, their sobs echoing in the room. The pain and sadness of the moment overwhelm them, their tears mingling as they cry together. The embrace is filled with the unspoken words of love, gratitude, and the heartbreak of dreams left unfulfilled.

In that shared embrace, they find a fragile solace amidst the turmoil. The decorations, the cold dishes, and the twinkling lights become witnesses to their shared grief and the silent promises they had made to each other. Their hearts,

though broken, are bound together by the deep love and respect they have for one another.

Farhan's heart aches with a pain so profound, yet he finds strength in Zainab's embrace. He knows that he must let go of his dreams, but in this moment, he cherishes the bond they share. The future remains uncertain, but the love and memories they have created will forever be a part of their story.

As time passes, Zainab finds herself in a deeply emotional and conflicted state. The partition, a cruel twist of fate, had torn her apart from her first love, Ayaan. His reappearance has reignited feelings she thought she had buried long ago. The memories of their love, the promises they made, and the dreams they shared come rushing back, overwhelming her heart and mind.

Yet, standing by her side through her darkest times has been Farhan. His unwavering support and kindness, his constant presence and care, have built a strong bond between them. Farhan has been her rock, her shoulder to lean on when the weight of the world felt unbearable. His love for her has grown quietly but deeply, a love nurtured through shared pain and silent understanding.

Zainab's heart is torn between two loves. On one side, there's Ayaan, the man who was her first love, whose words and promises still echo in her mind. The

fire of partition had separated them, but her feelings for him remain strong, like a flame that refuses to be extinguished. On the other side, there's Farhan, the man who has stood by her, loved her selflessly, and offered her a new hope for the future.

She feels an overwhelming sadness as she contemplates her decision. The weight of her emotions presses down on her, making it difficult to breathe. The memories of Ayaan and the moments they've shared are precious to her, yet the thought of losing Farhan, who has become an integral part of her life, fills her with an indescribable sorrow.

Zainab's tears flow freely as she wrestles with her heart. The room feels heavy with the tension of her unspoken dilemma. She wishes she could find a way to honor both loves, to hold onto the past while embracing the future. But the choice looms before her, a decision that will shape her life and the lives of those she holds dear.

In that fragile moment, she realizes that her choice is not just about choosing between two men. It's about choosing a path for herself, about finding a way to move forward with grace and strength. The love she feels for both Ayaan and Farhan is real, but in different ways. Her heart aches with the weight of this realization, knowing that no matter what she chooses, a part of her will always carry the pain of the path not taken.

Zainab stands on the precipice of her decision, her heart a battlefield of conflicting emotions. Her tears, a testament to the depth of her love and the intensity of her pain, continue to fall as she contemplates the path ahead.

The room is silent, save for the sound of her quiet sobs, as she prepares to make one of the most difficult choices of her life.

As the days turn into weeks, Ayaan's condition begins to improve significantly. Farhan takes care of him with unwavering dedication, tending to his every need. Zainab watches from the sidelines, her heart heavy with confusion and sorrow. The sight of Farhan selflessly caring for Ayaan only deepens her internal turmoil, as she grapples with the complex emotions swirling within her.

One day, Farhan enters Zainab's room, holding a stack of papers in his trembling hands. His heart is pounding, his mind a whirlwind of conflicting thoughts. He musters a fragile, fake smile, but it barely conceals the profound sadness he feels inside. "Zainab," he says, his voice barely above a whisper, "these are the divorce papers. I've already signed them... I think it's time you do too."

His hands shake as he extends the papers towards her. The weight of the moment is almost unbearable, and he feels as though he's breaking apart from the inside. Each breath he takes is filled with pain, each word laced with heartbreak. The smile he wears is a mask, hiding the tears that threaten to spill over.

Zainab looks at the papers, her own emotions a tumultuous sea. She sees the trembling in Farhan's hands, the sadness in his eyes. The room feels heavy, the air thick with the unspoken pain and sorrow they both share. Zainab's heart aches as she realizes the depth of Farhan's sacrifice, his love, and the agony he must be feeling.

Tears well up in her eyes as she takes the papers from him. The weight of the decision before her feels like a crushing burden. Farhan's fake smile falters, and a single tear escapes, trailing down his cheek. He feels his heart breaking, the dreams he once held now slipping away into the shadows.

Without a word, Zainab wraps her arms around Farhan, holding him close. Their shared sorrow spills over, and they cry together, their tears mingling as they embrace. Farhan's facade crumbles, his sobs wracking his body as he clings to Zainab. The pain of letting go, the anguish of unfulfilled dreams, and the love they both feel but cannot express pour out in that moment.

Zainab clutches the divorce papers, her heart heavy with emotions. Tears well up in her eyes, and with a trembling voice, she says, "No, Farhan. I... I cannot I won't leave you. I will always be by your side." Her words resonate with a mixture of determination and sorrow, a promise made in the depths of her heart.

They embrace, and both break down, their tears mingling as they cry together. The room fills with the sound of their shared grief, their sobs echoing off the walls. The weight of their emotions, the love they have for each other, and the pain of their predicament overwhelm them.

After a while, Farhan manages to gather his strength. With gentle hands, he wipes away Zainab's tears and softly brushes her hair away from her face. His touch is tender, filled with the care and love he has for her. "No, Zainab," he says, his voice steady yet choked with emotion. "Ayaan is your true love. The one you have fought for all this time. Now, the time has come for you to be with him."

His words carry a mixture of resignation and love, a final act of selfless sacrifice. Zainab's heart aches as she hears him, the depth of his love breaking her heart

even more. She knows that Farhan's love for her is true and pure, but she also knows that his words come from a place of genuine care for her happiness.

Farhan, holding back his tears, takes a deep breath and looks into Zainab's eyes, his heart heavy with the weight of what he is about to say. "Zainab," he begins, his voice breaking with emotion, "you need to go to Ayaan. This isn't your fault. Ayaan has lost everything. Now, you are the only person he has left. For the past two years, he has fought through his life, waiting for this moment. He deserves to have his love by his side."

Tears stream down his face as he continues, "Ayaan has sacrificed so much, and now it's time for him to find happiness with you. I know how much you mean to him, and I see how much he means to you. This is your chance to be together, and I can't stand in the way of that."

Farhan's voice trembles as he says, "You loved Farhan, and Farhan loved you. We came together because of circumstances, but now, you must follow your heart." His words hang heavy in the air, filled with the heartbreak of unfulfilled dreams and the love he knows he must let go.

Despite his resolve, Farhan can't hold back his own tears. He feels the pain of his sacrifice deep in his soul, a wound that may never fully heal. The sadness

and heartbreak overwhelm him, and he weeps openly, his sobs echoing through the room.

Zainab, her own heart breaking, wraps her arms around Farhan once more. They hold each other tightly, their tears mingling as they cry together. In that moment, they share a sorrow so profound, a bond forged in the depths of their love and sacrifice.

The room, filled with the remnants of Farhan's efforts to create a beautiful anniversary celebration, now bears witness to their shared grief. The decorations, the cold dishes, and the twinkling lights become silent observers of their heartbreak.

In their embrace, Farhan gently brushes Zainab's hair away from her face, his touch tender and filled with love. "You deserve to be happy, Zainab," he whispers, his voice filled with a mix of love and resignation. "Go to Ayaan. Be with him. That is where your heart truly belongs."

Zainab nods through her tears, understanding the depth of Farhan's sacrifice. Her heart aches with gratitude and sorrow for the man who has stood by her side, offering her unwavering support and love. As they part, she knows that the

bond they share will forever remain, even if their paths now lead in different directions.

Farhan watches with a heavy heart as Zainab, her hands trembling, signs the divorce papers. The moment her pen touches the paper, it feels as though his entire world comes to a standstill. The weight of the finality crashes over him, and he can no longer hold back the tears. Both Farhan and Zainab's eyes well up, their tears flowing freely, a testament to the depth of their shared sorrow.

As Zainab finishes signing, Farhan's heart shatters. He feels an unbearable pain, a hollow ache that seems to consume him. Without thinking, he pulls Zainab

into a tight embrace, their tears mingling as they cry together. The room is filled with the sound of their shared grief, a poignant symphony of heartbreak and love.

Through his sobs, Farhan whispers, "Please, come see me when you need to. As long as there are stars in the sky, I will wait for you." His voice is choked with emotion, each word a struggle to get out. The promise hangs in the air, a bittersweet vow that speaks to the depth of his love and the pain of letting go.

Zainab clings to Farhan, her own heart breaking with the weight of their parting. The love and respect they have for each other are palpable, even in this

moment of profound sadness. Their embrace is filled with unspoken words, a silent acknowledgment of the bond they share and the sacrifices they have made.

In that fragile moment, they find a fleeting solace in each other's arms, knowing that their paths are now diverging. The tears continue to flow, each drop a testament to the love they had hoped to share and the dreams that will remain unfulfilled.

The day of Ayaan and Zainab's wedding finally arrives, a day filled with a mix of emotions, anticipation, and hope. The air is thick with the scent of fresh flowers, and the soft glow of lanterns casts a magical light over the venue. Friends and family gather, their faces reflecting the joy and excitement of the occasion.

Before the wedding begins, a significant moment unfolds. Farhan, with a heavy but determined heart, speaks to Zainab's family. He explains the depth of Ayaan and Zainab's love, urging them to give their blessings and allow the marriage to take place. His words are filled with sincerity and love for both Ayaan and Zainab, and his plea is met with understanding and acceptance. This act of selflessness adds to the emotional weight of the day, a testament to Farhan's character and the bond they all share.

As the ceremony begins, Ayaan stands at the altar, his heart pounding with a mixture of nerves and happiness. He has waited for this moment for so long, and now, it is finally here. The music swells, and the doors open to reveal

Zainab, dressed in a stunning bridal gown. The sight of her takes Ayaan's breath away.

Zainab steps forward, her heart racing as she walks down the aisle. Her dress flows gracefully around her, the intricate details shimmering in the light. She feels a mix of emotions—joy, love, and a touch of sadness for the journey that has brought her here. But as she looks at Ayaan, all her doubts melt away, replaced by the certainty of their love.

Ayaan's eyes fill with tears as he watches Zainab approach. She looks like a vision, a dream come true. The memories of their past, the struggles they have faced, and the love that has endured through it all come rushing back to him.

He feels a deep sense of gratitude and awe for the woman standing before him.

As Zainab reaches the altar, their eyes meet, and in that moment, the world fades away. It is just the two of them, bound by a love that has withstood the test of time. Ayaan takes her hand, his touch gentle and filled with reverence. "You look beautiful," he whispers, his voice choked with emotion.

Zainab smiles, her eyes glistening with tears. "Thank you," she replies softly, her heart swelling with love for the man standing before her. The ceremony continues, each vow a testament to their enduring love and commitment to each other.

As the ceremony progresses, the Qazi Sahib stands before them and begins the traditional Muslim Nikah rituals. The hall is filled with a profound silence as everyone listens intently. **"Kya aap ko ye Nikah qubool hai?"** the Qazi Sahib asks, his voice echoing through the room. Ayaan, his voice steady and full of

emotion, responds, **"Qubool hai."** The words resonate deeply, a declaration of his love and commitment. The Qazi Sahib then turns to Zainab and repeats the question, "Kya aap ko ye Nikah qubool hai?"

Zainab, her heart overflowing with love and gratitude, responds with a voice filled with conviction, "**Qubool hai.**" The hall reverberates with the sound of their vows, the collective murmur of approval and joy filling the air as the guests witness this sacred union.

As they exchange rings, Ayaan's hands tremble slightly, the weight of the moment pressing down on him. He slips the ring onto Zainab's finger, his heart overflowing with love and devotion. Zainab does the same, her touch tender and filled with promise. The words "Qubool hai, Qubool hai, Qubool hai" resonate through the hall, sealing their union with a sacred vow.

As the ceremony concludes, Ayaan and Zainab make their way to Farhan, their hearts brimming with gratitude and respect. Farhan stands a little apart, a soft smile on his face, his eyes reflecting both pride and a quiet sadness. For a moment, all three remain silent, the weight of their intertwined journeys hanging in the air.

Zainab steps forward first, her eyes shimmering with emotion as she reaches out to Farhan. Gently, she wraps her arms around him, and he embraces her with a warmth that feels both comforting and bittersweet. She whispers a soft, “Thank you,” the words carrying the depth of everything he has sacrificed. Farhan's hand rests on her shoulder, a silent promise that he will always be there for her, even as her life takes a new path.

Ayaan approaches next, his eyes filled with respect and gratitude. He, too, hugs Farhan, feeling the strength of a man who has given so much for love. In that embrace, Ayaan silently vows to honor Farhan's sacrifice, to protect and cherish Zainab with all his heart.

As they pull away, the three share a lingering glance, one that speaks of unspoken promises, forgiveness, and love that is selfless and pure. In that fleeting moment, the air seems to hold its breath, capturing the beauty of a bond that transcends words—a bond woven through sacrifice, compassion, and the strength to let go.

Perhaps... in Another world... Another life...
We'll dance in the rain , As long as there are stars in the sky,

In the grand rainbows of life, love emerges as a force that defies logic and defies control—a fire that burns without permission, a fragrance that fills the air

even when one tries to ignore it. It blooms suddenly, without warning, like a wildflower in the midst of an untamed forest, and yet, it's as delicate as a morning dew that fades as dawn arrives. Love chooses its own time, its own path, and once it grips the heart, it leaves an undeniable mark that lingers long after it departs.

Yet, as intoxicating as it is, love does not bind itself to the happy endings we dream of. We hold on, hoping against hope, only to learn that love alone cannot guarantee a future. Life's harsh reality is that we must move forward, carrying the fragments of what was, because true zindagi—real life—is about growth, about embracing the unknown ahead rather than the longing that dwells behind. And so, we learn to move forward, even when our heart insists on staying in a memory.

In this journey, we realize that we don't always get what we desire instead, we get what destiny has written for us, and perhaps that is the most poetic cruelty of all. Moving forward, though it feels like leaving a part of ourselves behind, is the essence of life. We carry the ache, the memories, and the quiet whispers of what could have been, yet we walk on, for zindagi—life—is a river that flows ceaselessly, urging us to meet new horizons, however uncertain, however bittersweet.

"I promise, as long as the stars shimmer in the night sky , and the moon graces us with its light, love will continue to bloom in hearts, defying all logic and reason."

ꝒꝒꝒ

Dear Readers,

Thank you from the bottom of my heart for taking the time to read my novel. Your support and enthusiasm mean the world to me. It is your engagement

with the story that breathes life into these pages, and I am truly grateful for your presence on this journey. I hope the characters and their experiences resonated with you as much as they did with me.

With heartfelt appreciation,
Kahef Tauqeer

ꝒꝒꝒ

About The Author

Kahef was born on February 4, 2001, and brought up in the culturally rich city of Prayagraj. From an early age, Kahef exhibited a profound love for reading, immersing themselves in books with an insatiable curiosity. This passion was nurtured by a supportive family, who played an integral role in Kahef's

academic journey.

In 2023, Kahef graduated with a degree in Computer Science, having pursued their studies with dedication and a keen sense of purpose. Currently, Kahef is furthering their education, driven by a desire to expand their knowledge and expertise. Their journey reflects a beautiful blend of academic excellence and an unwavering commitment to their passions.

Kahef's love for reading and storytelling ultimately led to their debut as an author, with the enchanting book "The Echoes of Silent Separation." This work is a testament to their creative spirit and ability to craft compelling narratives.

Email : kaheftauqeer79@gmail.com
Inst : @kahef01

www.ingramcontent.com/pod-product-compliance
Lightning Source LLC
LaVergne TN
LVHW041100150826
845673LV00007B/1851

* 9 7 9 8 8 9 6 3 2 6 5 4 0 *